THE
BENEFITS
OF BEING
AN OCTOPUS

THE
BENEFITS
OF BEING
AN OCTOPUS

ANN BRADEN

Sky Pony Press
New York

First Edition

This is a work of fiction. Names, characters, places, and incidents are from the author's imagination and used fictitiously.

Sky Pony Press books may be purchased in bulk at special discounts for sales promotion, corporate gifts, fund-raising, or educational purposes. Special editions can also be created to specifications. For details, contact the Special Sales Department, Sky Pony Press, 307 West 36th Street, 11th Floor, New York, NY 10018 or info@skyhorsepublishing.com.

Sky Pony® is a registered trademark of Skyhorse Publishing, Inc.®, a Delaware corporation.

www.skyponypress.com

10 9 8 7

Library of Congress Cataloging-in-Publication Data is available on file.

Cover design by Kate Gartner
Cover illustration © Paul Oakley

Print ISBN: 978-1-5107-3748-8
Ebook ISBN: 978-1-5107-3752-5

Printed in the United States of America

For my mom

The history of the octopus illustrates the brain's ability to evolve. As they lost their ancestors' protective shells they were forced to become more intelligent.

—*The Octopus: Graceful Cephalopod of the Deep*
by Derby King

THE
BENEFITS
OF BEING
AN OCTOPUS

CHAPTER 1

I settle onto the couch with the chocolate pudding I saved from Friday's school lunch. This silence is amazing. Well, it's not complete silence—Hector is spinning the whirring dragon on his baby seat while he eats Cheerios—but it's pretty close. I savor a spoonful of pudding. How long do I have before Bryce and Aurora burst out of our bedroom arguing about something? When I left them in there Aurora was pretending to be Bryce's cat, and he was pretending to feed her milk, but that can't last. I mean, they're four and three. That's not how it works. I take another bite with my eye on the bedroom door, but it stays closed.

This never happens.

I glance down at my backpack. My debate prep packet is inside, and I'm actually tempted to work on it. I'm not a kid who does homework. And I definitely don't do big projects, which usually require glitter and markers and poster board and all sorts of things. None of which I have. Plus, last year in sixth grade, when I actually turned in a poster project, Kaylee Vine announced to the whole class, "Everyone! Alert the authorities! Zoey Albro turned in a project. The world must be ending." Then she made that *ahgn ahgn ahgn* sound like a fire drill, and did it every time she passed me in the hall for the whole next week.

But this project doesn't need any glitter. And everyone else won't have fancy poster boards with foam letters that make my flimsy piece of newsprint that the teacher gave me look like gray toilet paper. All I need is to know something—and I do. And maybe, just maybe, if I do this—and if I can rock it—all the other kids will have their minds blown, and it'll be completely satisfying to watch. "Who would have guessed," they'll say, "that Zoey knew so much cool stuff? I had no idea! I thought I knew who she was, but clearly I didn't *at all.*" Maybe Kaylee Vine would even stop holding her nose and switching seats on the bus to get away from me.

I take out the debate prep packet and lean over the coffee table. *Which animal is the best? Support your selection with as many details as possible, including what it takes to survive in a variety of situations.* Ms. Rochambeau, the social studies teacher, says this debate will help us understand the debates that led up to the Civil War, and Mr. Peck, the science teacher, says it'll be a good assessment of all the work we've been doing about animals.

And the thing is, I already know which animal is best. The octopus. When Bryce was a tantrumming toddler and Aurora was a baby, we moved four times over the course of that year. But the one constant was this little TV/DVD combo that we toted around with us and an old DVD from the library free shelf: *The Mysterious and Fascinating World of the Octopus.* That DVD would send Bryce into an instant trance, and we watched it so often that I happily memorized every word of it.

Then, last year, when I couldn't go on the sixth grade field trip to the aquarium in Boston (my mom kept "forgetting" to send in the payment), Ms. Giddings, the guidance counselor, brought me back a book on octopuses.

And actually, "octopuses" is correct. You don't have to say "octopi" if you don't want to. The book told me so.

I find a pencil nub at the bottom of my backpack and start filling in the blanks with awesome things. Like their ability to instantly camouflage themselves, which they're amazing at because they have these things called *chromatophores*—that word was in my book—so the color of their skin can change to match what's around them. They even have muscles that change their skin's texture. Of course, it means that when they get mad or nervous they turn red and pimply, but nothing's perfect, right?

Ms. Rochambeau will be as surprised as anyone else when I stand up for the debate and use a word like *chromatophore*.

I settle deeper into the couch. If this were a regular Sunday (or really, any day), Frank would be here, watching TV (usually angry news guys). Frank is Lenny's dad, and Lenny is the owner of this trailer. Lenny is also my mom's boyfriend, and that's why we get to live here with his nice curtains and end tables that are perfectly aligned with this couch. Lenny even has an alphabetized DVD collection. He also has a recliner that Frank sits in like he's glued to it.

But today Frank went out for a walk to check the tree damage from a recent ice storm, and since Lenny and my mom are both at work, Hector and I get the main room of the trailer to ourselves. So even though Ms. Rochambeau announced that we needed our completed packet to be part of the debate, this time I can actually do it. This time I don't have to be counted out.

I'm three pages into the four-page packet when Hector starts throwing the Cheerios all over Lenny's nice carpet.

I get down on the floor so I can pick them up. "Those are for eating. Not for throwing," I tell him, but he keeps throwing them anyway. I remove his ammunition, so naturally he starts screaming. Then—since Hector's scream seems to work like the Bat signal—Bryce and Aurora burst out of our bedroom door, trampling all the Cheerios in their path. Bryce is yelling about his imaginary Bucket of Doom. Aurora climbs into my lap and covers her ears.

If I were an octopus, things would be so much easier. I'd have one arm to wipe Aurora's nose. Two more for holding both kids' hands when I pick them up from the Head Start bus stop to keep Bryce from wandering into the street after some rock he's spotted. One to hold Hector and his diaper bag on the afternoons when my mom works at the Pizza Pit. One to adjust my shirt because it doesn't really fit and it can get too revealing if I'm not paying attention, and I don't want to be "that girl." One so I could do my homework at least some of the time if I wanted. One to pick up the Cheerios that are always on the floor. And the last one to swipe a can of Easy Cheese from the Cumberland Farms convenience store. Because little snowmen out of Easy Cheese are the most magical thing little kids have ever seen. And Easy Cheese letters on a saltine is *totally* different than having to eat regular saltines. Aurora knew the letter *A* before she even turned two, thanks to Easy Cheese letters.

The main door opens and I hear Lenny stamping the snow off his boots in the hallway. I drop my debate packet into my backpack and get the rest of the Cheerio dust scraped into my hand as fast as I can.

"How's my baby?" Lenny booms as he comes around the corner into the main room. He pats Hector on the head, and then heads to the fridge to get a soda.

Lenny is Hector's dad. He's not Bryce and Aurora's dad. That was Nate. Nate used to take me hunting, which was cool. No meat tastes as good as the stuff you've caught yourself. But Nate's not around anymore. And my own dad was gone long before I could throw Cheerios. My mom doesn't seem to think he's worth talking about too much, but you never know . . . maybe he secretly liked documentaries as much as I do.

It's all okay though, because I like football, too, and so does Lenny. Plus, tonight is a playoff game and when my mom gets home from her shift, she's going to make her bacon-wrapped hot dog bites. Those are what got us Lenny in the first place. Maybe they'll make up for all the other stuff.

That evening my job is to keep Bryce and Aurora in our bedroom so they don't grab the bacon-wrapped hot dog bites before they're cooked. With Hector balanced on my hip, I position myself as a human shield near the door while simultaneously keeping my eye on Lenny's nice lamp, ready to leap for it if necessary.

Hector sucks hard on his pacifier as he watches Bryce and Aurora launch their plastic battlebots into the blanket "volcano." But then Bryce picks up Aurora's precious stuffed sea turtle, Petunia, as the next sacrifice, and Aurora starts shrieking at the top of her lungs to stop him. That's one benefit of living in a town like this—when the rich people donate their old stuffed animals, you can end up with an awesome sea turtle that even has a fact printed on the tag about the dangers of shrimp nets. And anyway, we're not as poor as we used to be. We're living in Lenny's trailer now. I mean, it's a really nice lamp.

I hear the clang of a spoon against the bowl as my mom mixes the barbecue sauce, the second-to-last step before the bites go in the oven. That means just a few more minutes before we can leave this room and I can settle onto the couch like a boss to watch the game.

Unfortunately, I'm not the only one who can hear that spoon against the bowl. Both Bryce and Aurora have suddenly forgotten all about the volcano.

"Bacon bacon wap!" Aurora shrieks.

Bryce makes a break for the door.

Instantly, I'm in full-on barricade mode. "You're not eating one until they're cooked—just like everyone else." I don't need to remind them what happened the last time my mom made these. The barbecue sauce stain on Lenny's wallpaper doesn't let anyone forget.

Bryce is trying to push me out of the way using every bit of his scrawny four-year-old arms, but I am immovable. Plus, Hector is helping to weigh me down.

"No fair, Zoey!" Aurora wails. "What if they're all gone?"

"There'll be one for each of you when they're ready."

Aurora puts on her "sour eyes" face. "I don't bewieve you."

"Trust me. Both of you will get a bacon-wrapped hot dog bite." I pry Bryce's hands off of my sweatshirt, but he keeps pushing on me with his head like a silent slow-motion ram. "I promise!"

Bryce stops his ramming and looks up. "Pinky promise?"

I nod and hook my pinky around his. "Pinky promise."

It's only when I hear the oven door closing shut and the beeps of my mom setting the timer on the stove that I release them. "Remember," I whisper, pulling them close before they can zoom by me. "No yelling, no running, no messes."

Magically, they settle right down on the far side of the living area and start playing quietly with their toy cars. The promise of a bacon-wrapped hot dog bite is a powerful thing.

Frank is back in his recliner. The pregame show is on, but even though we've lived with him and Lenny for a whole year and a half I don't know if he even likes football. I don't know if he actually likes anything. He's like a beetle propped belly-up, especially if that beetle is the kind that spends most of the time with either a cigarette stuck in its mouth or a strand of cinnamon-flavored floss hanging from its teeth. One's healthier than the other, but both are gross.

I sidle up to my mom in the kitchen area, but she doesn't thank me for my heroic feat of keeping the kids out from underfoot. She just takes Hector from me. "He needs a bath," she says.

I hear Lenny in the entryway, coming in from outside. He went out to check on his car an hour ago, and I bet he ended up talking to everyone in the trailer park. Everyone knows Lenny, and everyone loves Lenny.

He strides across the living area into the kitchen, the frigid January air still clinging to him. "How's my pair of cuties?" he says to my mom and Hector. His voice is loud enough for him to still be talking to the neighbors. He takes Hector from her and bends down with him so they can peer into the oven window. "And look what's in there! You see how she wrapped up each hot dog bite real tight, Hector? That'll make sure each bite begins and ends with bacon. And they're going to come out nice and crispy because your mommy knows to take them out at the exact right time to add the extra barbecue sauce."

My mom stops drying her hands to give a little laugh and a curtsy. Maybe making these will remind Lenny why he got together with her in the first place. She used to tell great jokes, too, ones that would have Lenny doubled over laughing at her impressions, but it's been a long time since she told one.

Once the coin toss starts the game, Lenny gives Hector back to my mom and settles onto the couch with his soda (he never drinks beer) and the giant tub of cheese puffs he gets from Walmart just for football games. I sit down next to him, and he hands me the cheese puffs without a word. I like that—how it's just understood that I get to hold them.

My mom disappears with Hector into the bathroom for his bath, but that's okay. Patriots' games are my time with

Lenny anyway. Not only do I get to hold the cheese puffs, but if there's some football rule I don't get—like knowing where the defenders' hands can't be when a receiver is trying to catch the ball—then Lenny explains it. Both of us are always on the edge of the couch for every third down, me eating those cheese puffs and him drinking his soda. Basically, it's the best time ever.

By the time the game gets under way Bryce and Aurora have shifted to right in front of the TV, but they still only pay attention for commercials, when it's "more fun." Mostly they're zooming the toy cars around, pretending they're trying to outrace the Death Star (they haven't seen the movie yet, so they don't exactly get it).

"Come on, defense!" Lenny mutters. "You got this."

"Let's get a sack right here," I say, leaning forward.

Lenny nods and takes a swig of soda without taking his eyes off the screen. "That's right. Push 'em out of field goal range. Listen to Zoey."

We watch as the Colts hike the ball and our defensive linemen close in on the quarterback. The pocket's closing around him, and then—ooh! Even better! It's a fumble!

"Yes!" Lenny yells, pumping his fist in the air as the refs unpack the pile of players and signal the Patriots now have possession.

Lenny and I high-five, and then I lick the orange cheese dust off my fingers in celebration. This is how things are supposed to be. I've got a nice couch to sit on—which, thanks to

Lenny, is perfectly centered in the room—cheese puffs to eat, and a great game to watch.

At halftime, when no one's looking, I reach into my backpack for my debate packet and slip it into my front hoodie pocket. I'll finish it after the game.

But when I look up, I realize that when I wasn't paying attention, Bryce and Aurora got so excited about a commercial that they started hurling toy cars at the TV. Before I can stop them, Frank erupts from the depths of his recliner.

"THROW ONE MORE STUPID CAR AT MY TV, AND I'LL POUND YOU INTO THE GROUND!"

He keeps shouting, and it's like watching an ancient, wrinkled mountain explode, revealing an interior that's straight-up burning, swear-filled lava. Bryce and Aurora scream and run into our bedroom, tripping over each other as they go.

They slam the door shut, and I hate myself. Because in the far back corner of my mind, a horrible part of me is glad that I can watch the rest of the game in peace.

That's when the power goes out.

Of course it does.

Next to me, Lenny stands up and immediately trips over the coffee table. My mom bursts in from the bathroom, using her phone as a flashlight and carrying a soaking wet Hector on her hip.

Lenny calls over to her, "You got any guesses why we're in the dark?"

But she doesn't say anything. She just heads for the oven and takes out the bacon-wrapped hot dog bites. "I'm sorry. Hopefully, they'll still be crispy." She props the phone/flashlight under her chin, hefts Hector up higher on her hip, and transfers the hot dog bites onto a plate with a spatula.

They smell amazing. Like the pig is roasting on a spit right in the living room, dripping delicious grease all over the carpet.

Lenny makes his way into the kitchen as my mom pours the rest of the barbecue sauce over the top of them. He pops one in his mouth, and then shakes his head. "I've had better."

"I—I'm sorry," my mom stammers. "And I'm sorry you can't watch the rest of the game."

Lenny takes the plate of hot dog bites and shrugs. "I'll watch it at Slider's."

And with that, Lenny and the plate are out the door, and I'm left sitting on the couch.

No Lenny.

No game.

No bacon-wrapped hot dog bites. And I'd promised.

CHAPTER 2

Frank starts that old man snore of his—because he always goes to sleep the instant the TV goes off. In the kitchen, my mom works to scrape the burned bits of bacon off the baking sheet. "Zoey, can you go check on Bryce and Aurora?"

Oh, look. She hasn't forgotten that I exist.

"Shouldn't someone go check the fuse box or something?" I say.

"I'm sure it's out everywhere. Go check on your brother and sister."

I push myself up off the couch and wind my way through the dark to the window. Pulling back Lenny's nice curtains makes it pretty clear that the rest of the trailer park is lit up all bright and showy.

"It's just us," I say.

"Zoey Albro! I asked you to check on them! Lenny's pans are going to be impossible to get clean later if I let this stuff harden."

Why are clean pans more important than a functioning fuse box? It's been a long time since my mom made any sense. At least the light from the other trailers makes it easier to walk across the rest of the living area.

When I push open the door to our bedroom, it's pitch-black and nothing seems to be moving.

"Bryce? Aurora?"

All I hear in response is a whimper coming from their bed.

I quickly make my way through the dark, stepping on battlebots and other little plastic toy parts as I go. I hear the whimper again.

"Bryce?" I put my hand out toward the sound and find him. He's trembling. I hear a muffled sob and feel Aurora lying next to him. She's shaking, too.

"We . . . we . . . " Bryce starts, but his words disappear into a hiccup.

"Are you guys okay?"

Another hiccup. More whimpering.

"What's wrong?" I say.

"We . . . we can't see!" Bryce finally sobs. "We can't see anymore!"

I let out a long breath. They're not hurt. They're not sick.

"Is it because we got Frank mad at us?"

I squeeze each of their hands. "Oh, you sillies, it's just that the power is out. Your eyes still work fine." I crawl across the bed to get to the window and pull the curtains to the side. "See? You can see the icicles coming off of the neighbor's roof, right?"

In the glow from the neighbor's motion-sensor porch light, I can make out their faces. Bryce is biting his lip, but it keeps quivering anyway. Aurora has Petunia the Sea Turtle in a death grip and is sucking on one of her flippers. Their eyes are still fixed in a state of terror. My mom and I have gone through the power going off plenty of times, but Bryce and Aurora were too little to remember. What are they supposed to think when all the lights go out—when suddenly there's no Mickey Mouse night-light and no warning?

Bryce turns toward Aurora and wraps his arm around her, his nose buried in her hair. "At least we get hot dog bites."

I try to swallow, but it catches in my throat.

Aurora sniffs and looks at me. "You gonna tell us when they ready?"

Her eyes. Why do her eyes have to be so hopeful?

"Guys, I'm so sorry . . . There aren't any hot dog bites for us."

Aurora lets out a wail.

Bryce shuts his eyes, curls into a ball, and covers his ears with his hands. "No! No! No! No!"

I slide in next to them so I can wrap them both up tight.

They both instantly burrow into me, Aurora at my shoulder and Bryce's head driving into my stomach.

"I'll tell you a story instead, okay?" I say.

I never knew I could tell stories—or 'tories as Aurora says—until one day when Bryce had woken up from one of his nightmares and couldn't get back to sleep no matter how much I rubbed his back. I had made up stories all the time before that to get myself out of trouble—like having to explain to my mom how I ended up with a new can of Easy Cheese from Cumberland Farms—but bedtime stories? Not so much. Thankfully, Bryce and Aurora don't exactly care (or know) that I'm just making it up as I go along. And telling stories means I get to spend time in a world where the person in charge of what happens is me.

Tonight I start with three kids who live in a castle and don't have electricity, and I go from there. And who cares if I take some parts from the Batman movie and some parts from a documentary I once watched about Genghis Khan? The main thing is that the kids triumph over evil *and* that Bryce and Aurora both fall asleep.

After they're both breathing evenly, I stay where I am, lying between them, staring out at those icicles. They're like teeth waiting to chomp someone. Because the problem is that real life isn't like a story—I'm not in charge, and it's usually the good guys who get chomped.

But if I were an octopus, those icicles wouldn't get me. I would squish my body into a ball and jet away—fully camouflaged, of course.

I slither out from Aurora's arms, find a pencil on the floor, and take the debate packet out of my pocket. I only have one page left, and I position myself at the window so I can use the neighbor's porch light. I go back and forth about whether it's a good thing that a baby octopus starts out life the size of a pencil eraser, because the eraser on my pencil is pretty darn small. But I decide to include it because anything that can start out floating around defenseless in the ocean that size—and then defeat the odds to grow into this powerful creature—has to mean business.

I fill out those remaining blanks. Every single one.

Just as I finish, the front door slams and I hear Lenny's voice. There's some fumbling around and a thump like Lenny might have just smashed his toes on something. He curses.

"I'm so—sorry," I hear my mom stammer.

"Well, it sure isn't my fault we're in this mess," Lenny snaps.

I can totally believe it's my mom's fault. Recently it's like she can't do anything right.

"I thought I filled out the form right. I thought for sure we'd get approved for assistance—" my mom starts.

Lenny interrupts her before she can say anything more. "In there."

I don't know what he's talking about until I hear their bedroom door shut, and I realize they've disappeared inside it. They almost never argue about money or bills or anything really when I can overhear them.

The neighbor's light goes out, and I'm back to being completely in the dark.

In so many ways.

So it wasn't the fuse box—it was the power company who cut us off. In our old life, Mom got really good at filling out the form for financial assistance to take care of it. But she hasn't exactly been a take-care-of-it mom for a while now.

And she sure isn't the one left holding Aurora and Bryce when everything falls to pieces.

I take a deep breath. An octopus might start out defenseless, but it sure doesn't stay that way.

On a wave of octopus arms, I roll across our bedroom, sliding around the battlebots, checking the distance to my mattress so I don't trip over it, and simultaneously reaching for the doorknob with one of my tentacles. I silently roll across the main room, my skin changing to match snoring Frank and his recliner as I pass by. Just around the corner, in the entryway, the washing machine sits up against the wall. It's broken (except for when it pretends to work and turns all of our clothes gray), but that doesn't matter now. I scale it, one sucker at a time, until

I'm on top of it, right next to the section of wall that got all soft from a leak awhile back. Right where Bryce's lightsaber made a hole last summer when he and Lenny were play-fighting. It's a hole that leads right into my mom and Lenny's bedroom, and my hunch was right: I can hear what they're saying from here. If I put my eye up against the hole I can even see them.

Because that's the thing about an octopus: it knows it needs to hide its soft, squishy body out of sight, but if anyone bothered to take a closer look at the hole in the reef, they'd see a big, unblinking octopus eye staring out at them.

Through the hole I can see Hector sitting in the middle of the bed, waving my mom's phone/flashlight around like a strobe light. Lenny is organizing his undershirt drawer with an actual flashlight, completely oblivious to the disco dance party room that he's in.

That's another thing about getting to live with Lenny in this trailer: it is seriously neat and tidy and organized. In our last apartment, pre-Lenny, the countertop was rotting around the edges, so you'd realize halfway through washing dishes that water had been pooling downstream into the carpeting. We basically spent our six months in that apartment ducking under the five clotheslines that crisscrossed the main room and smelling like we lived in a swamp.

Lenny's trailer, on the other hand, is the opposite of a swamp. His bathroom is the most non-moldy thing you've ever seen.

"I told you I delivered that form last week," he's saying. "You believe me, don't you?"

My mom, sitting near Hector on the bed, dodges to the left to avoid being whacked by her strobe light phone. "Of course I believe you."

Lenny starts laying his undershirts out on the bed to refold them. "You can't always blame someone else."

My mom bites her lip and looks away. "It's just that I spent a whole day on that form. I thought I filled it out right."

"But how would you even know if it's right?"

I want to look away. She didn't used to be this much of a mess. But I force myself to keep my octopus eye pressed against the hole, wide and unblinking. Why is she the one that all four of us kids are related to? Why can't it be Lenny instead? All confident and competent. No one at school would mess with me if I were like him.

"I—I know," my mom stammers. "But I asked Connor to look at it first, and he thought it—"

My mom's voice falters.

In the disco light, I can make out Lenny shaking his head. "Really? *Really?*" He stops folding and crosses the room to be right next to my mom. "You really showed all the private details about our lives to Connor?"

Connor waits tables at the Pizza Pit, too, and he's basically the only friend my mom has right now. He's also totally awesome, but Lenny never seems to be a big fan of his. I don't know if it's because Connor's gay or if it's because of something else.

Hector drops my mom's phone and starts crying. "I thought he could help," my mom says quickly. "He's not someone who would judge us or anything, and he doesn't get all flustered with forms like that and—"

Lenny hands my mom's phone back to Hector and then wraps his arms around my mom from behind. I remember him wrapping her up like this when they first got together and how she would close her eyes and lean her head against his shoulder like there was nowhere else to be in the world.

"We can take care of our own business ourselves," Lenny says. "You've got me taking care of you now."

My mom has her eyes squeezed shut, but it's not like before when she'd be looking all calm. It's more like how Bryce looked when he accidentally crashed into Lenny's tower of alphabetized DVDs, and he closed his eyes tight as if that'd make the mess he'd made go away.

I scoot down off the washing machine. I can't stand to see my mom's face looking like that. If she could do stuff right the first time around, it wouldn't have to be like this.

CHAPTER 3

In the morning I wake up to the sound of Lenny's car pulling out of the driveway. The electricity still isn't back on, but the sun (that rebel) has started to lighten the sky for free.

Another thing about Lenny is that he's never late to work. Even though his part-time job at the auto parts store has him leaving before seven, he's still on time. On time and as clean-shaven as you could possibly get. Between Lenny's obsession with his lather shaving brush and his insistence on paying attention to little details like clocks and his car's odometer, he's basically the exact opposite of my mom's other boyfriends with their varying degrees of scruffiness and whose main talents were eating all the food in our fridge.

Well, Bryce and Aurora's dad, Nate, wasn't bad. He was kind, and those times he took me hunting were super fun. But then he stopped hunting and started drinking, and you can't hold down a job and take care of kids when you're like that. He'd just look out the window of the camper van we lived in back then like the answer was out there. I mean, maybe it was, because my mom told him loads of times to go to AA meetings—but he never went.

Things went south between him and my mom one day when we were at the boat launch. He had been trying to convince Bryce to go swimming with him, but Bryce couldn't swim and Nate was drunk and didn't exactly remember that. Evidently, being yelled at by your girlfriend in front of your kids and a whole bunch of kayakers wakes up something inside you, and he drove off in the camper van and didn't come back.

I push myself up on my mattress until I can see Bryce and Aurora. Bryce had one of his nightmares last night, but you wouldn't know it from looking at him now. They're both still breathing deep like two little squirrely-haired Darth Vaders. I hate waking them up. It's like you've finally won the lottery of peace and quiet and then you rip that winning ticket to shreds and dump a bucket of angry, screaming monkeys on your head.

I pull on my own clothes and brush my hair, and then perch myself next to them on their bed and give them each a little nudge. "Bryce . . . Aurora . . . Time to get up."

Just a few years ago, my mom was the one waking me up. She'd sing this little good morning song even though she can't carry a tune. That was when she had to keep a bag of frozen corn on her face to numb the pain from rotting teeth—because some people have parents who remind them to brush their teeth, but my mom's didn't. Still, she was determined not to take ibuprofen because she was pregnant with Aurora and had heard it could hurt the baby. She finally had to sell our beat-up car to scrape together the money to get those teeth extracted. She got five of them pulled, but the worst was the week after that. Because there we were with no car, fifteen-month-old Bryce who was coming down with an ear infection, and Aurora about to be born—and two more teeth started throbbing.

That was before we found the octopus DVD. And that was definitely before Lenny saved the day and paid for a new set of teeth for my mom.

I give Bryce and Aurora each another nudge, but it's like trying to wake up two rocks. I start to pull the bedspread off them. Bryce grabs hold tight, curls into it, and growls. Monkeys growl sometimes, right? It can't always be *oo-oo-aa-aa*. Aurora, with her eyes still closed, pinches her face together tight.

"You got to get up," I say.

"You're not Mommy," Bryce growls back. "I don't have to listen."

"Not Mommy!" Aurora echoes.

Every day it's like this! Does it matter that it was me who told them a cool story last night? No.

"You know Mommy has to sleep in because she has to wake up for Hector in the night," I remind him.

I don't point out that she never stayed in bed like this when Bryce and Aurora were babies. I've peeked in on her enough mornings recently to know that she's probably lying in the fetal position and that if I ask when she's going to get up, she'll say, "Soon." But she won't. I've stopped hoping to see her before I leave for school. And being rejected like that is not what Bryce and Aurora need to start the day.

"You're not Mommy!" Bryce yells at the top of his lungs.

Screaming monkeys. Flippin' screaming monkeys.

Twenty minutes later, I've managed to get them out the door and to the corner of our road in the trailer park where the Head Start bus picks them up. Bryce is still in his pajamas, and Aurora insisted on wearing a skirt and a T-shirt even though it's January in Vermont. But they're both wearing winter coats, so that's something. And everyone brushed their teeth for at least a minute—that's one of my mom's nonnegotiable rules. And thankfully Frank kept sleeping through the whole thing.

When I'm finally on my way to my own bus stop, I see Silas come around the corner of his trailer. He's in seventh grade like me, and he and his dad have a good spot at the end of the row, so that when they look out the window on one side it's all trees.

"Hey," I call.

Silas glances up from under his camo trucker hat. "Hey," he says back. He climbs over a grey mound of snow left from the plows and catches up with me.

"What's up?" he asks.

Silas has the kind of freckles that make you want to connect the dots to form constellations and dragons and things. Other kids give him a hard time because heaven forbid if you're a boy and you have a habit of crying when you're sad. But he's nice.

Still, I'm not about to let my mouth run about not having electricity. "Not much," I say.

Silas kicks a chunk of ice, and it skids along the road. "Aren't you going to ask me?" he says.

"Ask you what?"

"What's up?" he says.

"Oh." I watch him as he plods forward in his steel-toed boots, his hands in his pockets and his eyes on the line of trees beyond the trailers. There's something about Silas that's different from anyone else I know. "What's up?" I ask.

"My dad and I went hunting this weekend." He drops his voice. "For bobcats."

I look around. "Why are you whispering? Is that illegal?"

He shakes his head. "Open season until the second week of February. It's just . . ." He pauses and glances at me like somehow we're part of some awesome conspiracy. "The bobcat is the most challenging game there is. Pure stealth. In the whole state only a couple dozen hunters will be successful this year."

"Why? Are they really rare?"

Silas keeps his eyes on the trees. "They're around. But you've got to be like a cat to find them. And there aren't as many places to track them now . . . You remember that big town meeting about guns last year?"

I nod. That meeting was one of the other rare times that Frank got out of his chair and left the house. He even took his .22 rifle down from the shelf, cleaned it, and put it back up before he went. He always keeps it there in case the government goes all "tyrannical." And he made Lenny go to the meeting, and Lenny made the rest of us go. It seemed like it was one bunch of people trying to tell another bunch of people what to do. And who likes being told what to do? Especially if the person doing the telling didn't grow up here and doesn't get how things have always been.

"Well, those anti-hunting people put No Trespassing signs up in their woods. But that doesn't mean we're going to give up," Silas says. "We tracked both sides of the public land along Squaretail Brook, all the way down that hillside to where it runs into the Beal River." He raises his eyebrows. "We didn't find a single sign of bobcat."

"Not even any tracks?" I say. "You must be bummed."

He shakes his head. "It's all part of the hunt. You've got to be just as stealthy as they are." He pauses. "Sometimes, a bobcat will match its steps to a coyote's tracks—will go footprint for footprint."

Maybe Silas is stealthy enough to figure out how to reconnect our electricity without the company knowing.

But it might have to be a bobcat-shaped electrical box for him to pay any attention to it. He's going on, now about what its scratch marks look like on trees. About how you have to keep your face to the wind when you're tracking. "Whatever bobcat is out there, it's one that knows how to hide, knows how to disappear."

"Too bad, man," I say.

Silas stops walking, looks at me, and gives that same weird "we're part of an awesome conspiracy" smile. "No. Not bad at all."

I stare at him. I picture his dad and him sitting in the front seat of their truck talking about bobcat tracks. They always seem so happy together. Like they're on the same team.

"Hey," I say. "Do you know where you file that form to get help with electricity and stuff like that?"

He stops and looks back at me. "I think my dad used to bring it to Family Services up on Route 14."

"Oh yeah. Thanks."

He nods and goes back to talking about the bobcat stuff. About how snow conditions are perfect because they prefer to be able to walk on hard-crusted snow, but this most recent dusting over that icy stuff will let him pick up its tracks. On and on.

Until we reach the bus stop—it's packed with kids older

than us and who look a whole lot less grimy than I do—and he clams up like he's never once heard of a bobcat. Because that's Silas's superpower: going for entire school days without talking. He's been doing it since the fifth grade when Brendan Farley got people to place bets about how quickly Silas would start crying, so he's really good at it by now.

Things would be a whole lot simpler if I could just build a wall around me like he does. I mean, I basically don't talk in class either, but it's so hard to keep my face blank when people are trying to mess with me.

I file onto the bus behind Silas and slide into the empty seat across from him. The bus is warm and quiet. But then I hear a voice behind me. It's Kaylee Vine making noises as if a pile of rotting fish was just deposited in her lap. "That smell," she says. Like she always does.

But not for long. I feel inside my backpack for my debate packet.

My stomach drops. Where is it?

"Ugh, I can't sit here anymore," I hear Kaylee say as she grabs her stuff and heads to the back of the bus.

My debate packet. Sitting at home. Still on the windowsill.

Why did I think today could be any different?

CHAPTER 4

I quickly pull my backpack closer to me and start drawing a cloud in the window's condensation. One circle. Two circles. Make it puffy. Puffier. Puffier. This cloud needs to be so big I can disappear inside it. Someplace where I can't hear Kaylee's voice.

The bus pulls away from the trailer park and starts heading down the street, where practically every house has a big yard, and some even have a swing set in back. I keep running my tentacle along the window, making the cloud bigger and bigger until there isn't any condensation left to draw in. It still isn't big enough.

The bus slows down for its next stop, and I peer through the wet window to see Matt Hubbard waiting up ahead. His bus stop is magically right in front of his house. No need to cross a whole trailer park. Instead, he gets to strut down his perfectly snowblown walk, probably after having waffles, an omelet, and several strips of bacon for breakfast, and probably after his mom gave him a kiss on the cheek and told him to "Have a good day, dear."

And certainly after he checked his backpack to make sure he had his homework.

I've seen his family before because they go out for pizza at the restaurant where my mom works—and they do that every single Saturday night. Every single one! It's like it doesn't matter if it's a payday week or not. Like they never run out of gas in the car and can't fill it up. Like it's easy for them all to be together at the same time with no one working or sick or totally stressed out or screaming or naked (that'd be Aurora).

It's like he lives on a beautiful tropical island, and I can see it and smell the pizza, but no matter how hard I swim I can't get there.

Matt gets on the bus, holds his trumpet case out in front of him so it can fit between the seats, and makes his way toward the back.

Even though we're in the same homeroom, he doesn't look my way. That's one of the things about the people on that beautiful tropical island: they can't see who's floating about in the ocean around them. Or maybe they can and they just choose not to look. I don't know.

I've never been there.

Fuchsia is waiting for me at my locker when I arrive. Fuchsia isn't her real name, but she wasn't a fan of the name McKenna, and she's even less a fan of her mom. She found out about the color fuchsia in second grade, and since all of first grade was kids coming up to her to order a McKenna and fries like she was a drive-thru window, she didn't look back.

Now she's leaning against the locker next to mine, her pink hair splayed out behind her. "I want you to know that I destroyed that white team yesterday."

"White team?" I drop my backpack and start opening my locker. "Are you talking about foosball? At the rec?"

She nods. "Destroyed."

"Who were you playing against?" I carefully tuck the edges of my winter jacket inside my locker so the sleeves don't get pinched. I love my jacket. Lenny gave it to me—it was this random present one day because it's my mom who buys our clothes, not him—and it's one of those camo jackets with the sleeves that look like leather but aren't really, and it's pink. It's awesome.

"I told you: the white team."

I eye her.

"And I destroyed them," she says. "Nine to nothing."

"You mean, you scored against a team of little plastic men

who were frozen in place with no one to spin their handles," I say.

"Nine times, baby."

I bite back a smile and shut my locker. "How long did that take?"

She shrugs. "Just a few hours, but I was persistent. And I had promised Jane Kitty I would bring home a victory."

Jane Kitty is a little scruffy ball of fur who followed Fuchsia home this past fall. I had been going on about Jane Goodall at lunch that day, and Fuchsia—who felt like living in the jungle would be way better than living with her mom—adopted the wild kitten as her own piece of jungle. I haven't gotten to meet Jane Kitty yet because my mom and Fuchsia's mom had a big blowup around the time we moved into Lenny's trailer, and we haven't been able to go to each other's places since. But Fuchsia talks about her all the time.

"Jane Kitty might be more proud of you if you could score against an actual opponent," I say. "How many points did I score against you last time?"

Fuchsia puts on a fake thinking face. "Hmm . . . I can't remember because it was *so long ago*."

"Well, I'm pretty sure I can remember your score. It started with a *z*, and—"

Fuchsia puts her finger to my mouth to stop me. "Sorry, you only get to talk smack if you're going to show up."

"I couldn't yesterday," I start to say. But Fuchsia is already heading down the hall.

"No show? No smack!" she calls.

Elementary school goes through sixth grade here, so this is our first year in middle school, and even though we're already halfway through the school year, I still haven't figured out the point of homeroom. Yeah, Mr. Bontaff takes attendance, but they take attendance during classes, too. And there's the morning announcements over the loud speaker about all the activities the good kids do like drama and jazz band, but that still leaves us eight and a half minutes of awkwardness. There aren't assigned seats, so I usually just try to find a seat in the back where no one will bother me. Unfortunately, I can't get there without walking past some girls who are going on about the animals they chose for the debate, and of course have their perfectly filled-out packets with them. The chromatophores right under my octopus skin switch to camouflage. When I slide into the seat, I might as well be made of the same colors as the desk and the metal chair legs.

I close my eyes. All I had to do was put the debate packet into my backpack. I could have done it last night when I finished it. I could have done it this morning before I woke up

Bryce and Aurora. I should have thought about it on my way to the bus stop. I still could have run back to get it. So what if Frank had woken up and yelled at me?

Most of the boys in my homeroom are bunched together like bees swarming an open jar of grape jelly. They're all buzzing—mostly about the Patriots' game yesterday—and it's like the jar of jelly is moving because soon the swarm is in the back corner right next to my desk. They're oblivious to me, of course, and I shift my backpack out of the way before it gets stepped on. The last thing I need is to be walking around with a giant footprint on my bag. I'd rather pretend that I'm not sure what people think of me instead of being forced to carry around physical proof of it.

"Come on," Brendan Farley is saying, "that was definitely the best play of the game. Did you see the look on that receiver's face when he dropped the ball? Priceless!"

Calvin Umbatoor shakes his head. "No way, man. It was the Pats' hurry-up offense in the third quarter. The Colts' defensive line didn't know what was coming at them."

Matt, with his trumpet-playing lungs, quiets them all down. "You're all wrong. The best play of the game was *clearly* the fumble on that third down in the first quarter and that's *because . . .*" He pauses for dramatic effect.

"Because the Colts were in field goal position," I mumble to my desk.

The sudden silence around me is the kind that makes me

lift my head without thinking. And there is Matt Hubbard looking right at me.

"Exactly," he says.

He's still looking at me.

My octopus chromatophores don't always listen to me. Suddenly, that oh-so-awesome camouflage skin has turned bright red and pimply all over.

CHAPTER 5

The "Social Studies and Science Interdisciplinary Block" arrives like a slow-motion steamroller.

The wall between the social studies and science classrooms has been opened. I'm on the social studies side because that's the class I would usually have now, but at least I can see the tanks of hermit crabs on the science side. They could use a cleaning. I'm signed up for extra help in science during the special Ace Period on Wednesdays because I don't do homework in that class either, but it's okay because Mr. Peck lets me spend the period cleaning the tanks. They're usually filthy. I figure he's the one who needs the extra help.

"Let's get crackin'!" Ms. Rochambeau calls out. "I want to see nothing on your desk except your debate packet. I'll be coming around to check."

Around me everyone moves in a flurry, clearing off their desks to leave only their beautiful, filled-out, remembered packets.

Octopuses can squish their bodies down to no bigger than a crumpled-up bag of chips. By the time Ms. Rochambeau gets to my desk I might as well be that balled-up bag, with all the chip bits eaten, ready to be tossed into the trash.

Ms. Rochambeau raises her eyebrows when she gets to me. Not in a "how clever to ball up like a bag of chips" way, but in that "you have disappointed me with your very being" way that teachers are so good at. She shakes her head as she writes my zero into her gradebook. "Sometime, Zoey, I hope you surprise me."

"I forgot it at home," I say to my desk. "I promise I finished it."

"Mm-hmmm," she murmurs. "It doesn't do you any good at home, unfortunately."

She pretends she believes me. I pretend I don't want to squirt octopus ink all over this classroom.

"Maybe I could be in the debate anyway," I say, even though she's already moved on to the next kid. "I know all my facts."

She doesn't look up from the other kid's packet. "Then you should have brought in your filled-out packet, so I could see that. I was very clear with my expectations."

Having to sit and watch everyone else is even worse than getting Ms. Rochambeau's Raised Eyebrow of Disappointment.

Calvin Umbatoor mumbles through his opening statement about the "terrifying *Tyrannosaurus rex*," reading directly from his packet. Then Matt Hubbard is up.

He stands up like he's been waiting his whole life for the opportunity to address the combined social studies and science classes. "My friends, the best animal on this earth is clearly the orca."

Did I make that whole Matt-agreeing-with-me-in-homeroom thing up? Did that even happen? Because part of me feels like I shouldn't be allowed to think the name Matt Hubbard—or, at least, that if I do, angry, flying Vikings will show up and beat me over the head with wooden swords, yelling "NOT WORTHY!" Because he's the whole package—like an all-expenses-paid trip to Disney World package. And I'm nothing like that. Maybe I'm the stub of an already used bus ticket—specifically the bus that my dad took to get away from us—and even then I'm the ticket stub that's at the back of the bus with muddy boot marks all over it.

But he did talk to me, didn't he? And he looked at me like he could see me and like he respected my amazing analysis of the Patriots' game.

Because it was amazing, wasn't it?

"They are fierce predators that can swim up to thirty miles per hour," Matt is proclaiming. He definitely isn't reading off his packet like Calvin was. "Orcas work together in teams to take down their prey. AND!" He raises his finger in the air.

"They will share the meat with the whole pod." In a flash he produces a giant bag of Swedish Fish and starts passing them out.

He keeps up his presentation over the joyful squeals as people get handfuls of candy fish delivered to their desks.

I pop one in my mouth. It's delicious.

Could I have actually competed with this?

"And they're camouflaged. Their black back blends in with the ocean if someone is looking down on them, and their white belly blends in with the sky if someone is looking up."

But two colors are nothing compared to the octopus's constantly changing camouflage. Right?

"And you're all eating fish right now, but they hunt and eat a wide variety of animals, including the seal, the sea lion, the stingray, the squid, and the octopus."

Right.

I stop eating the Swedish Fish.

Next Kaylee Vine stands up. Her shirt says I'M WATCHING YOU, and it's got a picture of an owl with giant eyes—and it fits her perfectly, like all of her clothes do.

"Owls are the best animal. They're wise and they have these things called light rods in their eyes so they can see every single leaf on a tree in the middle of the night. And they can rotate their head more than 180 degrees, so they can see everything around them."

There's something about the way Kaylee looks around at

everyone that makes me think she might be able to rotate her head more than 180 degrees, too. Under her watch no detail goes unnoticed. I realize my shirt has slipped to the side and I fix it. The downsides of a growth spurt means that my mom insists on buying clothes that are two sizes too big for me when she's at the consignment store.

"Their wings have a special pattern of interlocked feathers so they can fly silently through the air," Kaylee is saying. She isn't reading off her packet either.

I wouldn't have needed to look at my packet. I know my octopus facts cold. But still, Kaylee is saying this stuff like not only has she known it all her life, but like everyone with half a brain would know it, too. My leg starts twitching just imagining what it'd be like standing up there talking. Everyone would be looking at me. Even the owl on Kaylee's shirt.

"This means they can sneak up on unsuspecting chipmunks and grab them with their sharp talons. And before you get all upset about the chipmunks, you should know they're actually helping the chipmunk population. The strong chipmunks know how to take care of themselves. The owls are weeding out the ones who don't. And that's better for everyone."

I'm pretty sure it's not a coincidence that she looks straight at me when she says this.

Because if you can take care of yourself, you'd have clean clothes, and you wouldn't smell like cigarette smoke, and you'd definitely remember your debate packet. And how is it fair for the kids who are on top of stuff to have to share the classroom with kids who aren't?

"And, Calvin, I want you to know that I'll be coming for you and your T. rex's tiny little brain when we get to the Q&A part of this debate."

If I had remembered my packet and made the mistake of getting up there, that owl on Kaylee's shirt would be full-on rolling its giant eyes at me along with everyone else by this point. Did I really think Kaylee Vine was going to be impressed with my octopus facts? Did I really think she was going to give me a pass when the whole point of the debate is to prove everyone else wrong?

It's not enough to know your stuff. Not if one of the things you know for sure is that everyone you're going up against is better than you.

CHAPTER 6

After the school bus drops me off, I zip up my jacket and walk as quick as I can along the shoulder of Route 3. If I can get to the Pizza Pit before Bryce and Aurora's Head Start bus shows up, I can steal my favorite five minutes of the day. A logging truck whizzes past me, and I squint to block the spray of icy slush it kicks up from the road.

My mom's lucky to have this job. It's not as much money as the fancy place she worked in the tiny little mountain town of Peru, Vermont, where all the skiers came, but you can't keep a job like that if your car doesn't start when it's cold out. Plus, people eat at the Pizza Pit year-round, and we can walk there from the trailer.

When I arrive and push open the door, it's Connor who's holding Hector. They're standing just behind the pink neon

OPEN sign that's flashing on and off. Hector is giggling every time it turns on.

Ricky, the boss, has said it's okay if Hector's around a bit—says he makes it feel like a real family restaurant—just as long as he doesn't cry or make a mess, and only if it's during the half hour that my mom's and Connor's shifts overlap. And even though everything would be easier if my mom's shift started half an hour later so she wouldn't have to schlep him there until I could take over, I'd miss getting to see Hector and Connor together.

"Hey, Zoey," Connor says as soon as he sees me. "How was school today?" He's smiling his regular, giant smile. No one in the world could have a smile as great as Connor's.

"Where's my mom?" I ask, reaching to take Hector from him. "Do you need to take care of that table?"

Connor glances over at the booth of people. "Oh, they're fine. They've been here for hours, and they've got their check already . . . they don't need me." Connor reaches out and tickles Hector who's now squirming in my arms trying to get back to Connor. "But your mom needed me, didn't she, Mr. Cutiepie, because someone went and spit up all over her uniform and she had to go change."

"Was that you?" I say to Hector. My voice sounds awkward mimicking Connor's happy bubbliness, but Hector's eyes are wide and he keeps giggling. I'm pretty sure I usually talk to him like my mom does—mostly tired.

"Here." Connor gestures over to one of the booths. "Take a load off. I'll get you a water with lemon."

I settle onto the padded seat of the booth with Hector on my lap. He reaches for the rolled-up napkin of silverware and instantly throws it on the floor.

"I'm sorry," I say to Connor when he comes back over.

"No worries," he says, pocketing the silverware roll in the small black apron around his waist. "There are more where that came from." He sets down one ice water with a slice of lemon perfectly placed on the top of the glass—far enough away so it's out of Hector's reach—and one spoon close by. "That's for you, Mr. Cutiepie," he says, pointing to the spoon. "And the water is for your awesome older sister."

"Thank you," I say. I take a drink of the water while Hector is distracted by the spoon. I try to sneak a peek at Connor's tattoos. Ricky makes him wear a long-sleeve shirt under the standard black polo uniform, but you can still see the edges of them peeking out from the sleeve. He showed them to me once. There was one that looked like a cross with another cross inside it that he said he'd gotten when he was hiking around Peru. Like the country Peru. Not Peru the tiny town where our car wouldn't start. Connor made it all the way to a place where January is summertime.

"So, now," Connor says, sliding into the seat across from me, "let's get down to business. Which is better: an igloo with a marshmallow-roasting fire pit or a tree house in the jungle but you can only eat nuts?"

I lean back against the booth and bite back a smile. "The tree house in the jungle."

Connor raises his eyebrows. "Just nuts?"

"I like nuts."

He grins. "Okay. What have you got for me?"

"Let's see . . ." I close my eyes. "You have to walk across town when everything is black ice but you get to eat warm chocolate chip cookies the whole time? Or it's a beautiful day, but you have to spend it being chased by angry squirrels?"

Connor laughs out loud. "Oh, what a choice, Zoey." He considers for a minute. "Squirrels are fast. I'll take the cookies instead, and I'll ice skate the whole way."

Best five minutes of the day.

My mom comes out of the bathroom a few minutes later. She's kind of frazzled, still fixing her hair and stuff, but it's clear she's already switched over to work-mode mom. I like getting to sneak peeks at her waitressing, the way she can fly out of the kitchen carrying multiple plates of steaming pasta, the way she pushes buttons on the cash register like a boss, the way she writes down customers' orders in this cool, magical code and can do it without ever looking away from the customer. It's like waitressing is the one time when the competent mom I remember comes back and says hello.

She hands me the diaper bag. "At least there was an extra uniform shirt in there. You can't see the spot on my pants, right?"

Her black pants look the same as ever. I shake my head.

"Good." She turns to Connor. "Okay, what other prep work do I need to get done before the dinner rush?"

"I was able to mix up two of the salad dressings, but I didn't have time to get to the ranch yet . . . " Connor says as they push past the doors into the kitchen.

I look over at the table where Matt Hubbard's family always sits on their Saturday night dinners. Matt and his mom and his dad and his little sister—just like in a commercial. His sister is a few grades younger than us. She has some fancy name like Emmeline or Eleanor—or maybe it was just Emily, but she looked fancy and smart because she was always winning things, just like Matt, in elementary school—the spelling bee, the art contest for Earth Day, all that stuff. I bet they make up new contests just so the Hubbards can win them.

Like last week in homeroom when Mr. Bontaff made this whole big deal about how Matt had done such an amazing job for his trumpet solo in the jazz band concert. About how it was "magnificent" and "amazing." I can't even imagine having a teacher say things like that about me.

But even though I don't do after-school activities like he does and even though I'm grimy, he still talked to me this morning. And he still gave me Swedish Fish even though I didn't have my debate packet like everyone else.

And he has really nice brown eyes.

"Zoey! What are you still doing here?" My mom bursts back through the kitchen doors. "Bryce and Aurora will be getting off the bus any second!"

I look at the clock on the wall. "Shoot!" I scoot out of the seat, swing Hector onto one hip, and sling his diaper bag onto my opposite shoulder on top of my backpack. "I'm going!"

The door jingles on my way out, and I'm soon huffing it across the parking lot and along Route 3. Up ahead, on the opposite side of the street, I can see the people waiting for their kids. They're at the corner where Pratt Street comes in, where the bus is about to stop, where I should be standing right now. I pick up the pace, and Hector giggles as if a horseback ride from a horse that's hyperventilating is the best kind ever.

The bus comes around the corner and slows down to a stop. The cars that usually zip down this stretch of road come to a halt as the bus switches to its flashing red lights. I watch as Bryce and Aurora emerge from the bus door in the midst of the other kids, just like they always do. On the opposite side of the street from me.

The school bus's flashing lights have stopped, its stop sign is tucked back in, and traffic starts to move again.

The other kids are heading off with their grown-ups down Pratt Street toward the houses in that neighborhood—but Bryce and Aurora are still standing there, looking around.

I'm always right there, waiting for them. Always. Maybe we don't have dinner at a table every night. Maybe they have to get free lunch tickets and deal with all the same shame I had to deal with when I was first in school.

But at the end of the day, I'm always there to pick them up.

"Bryce! Aurora!" I call as I run. "I'm right here!" But as soon as the words leave my mouth, I regret it.

Because Aurora yells, "Zoey!" and starts running toward me.

Directly across the street.

As though all the cars around her are just bubbles that will pop if they touch her.

A car slams on its brakes and lays on the horn.

In the closest lane, another car skids to a stop, and the car behind it narrowly misses rear-ending it.

The blare of the horns is so loud that Aurora comes to an abrupt stop halfway across the road and covers her ears.

But when you're at bumper level in a sea of honking, it doesn't matter how much you cover your ears. Those bubbles are still way louder than they should be.

Aurora bursts into tears.

On the far side of the street Bryce is screaming and stamping his feet. He's not even looking at Aurora anymore—it's like he's gone rabid.

One of the drivers rolls down his window and yells, "What do you kids think you're doing?" He starts to roll his window back up but pauses when he looks at me. "And for God sakes, put a coat on that baby!"

I glance down to see Hector just in his pajamas. Hector, of course, has started crying, too, and it might just be because he's about to lose all of his fingers to frostbite. Where's my layer of protective octopus slime? Where are my eight tentacles to pull all three kids close to me and wrap them up so they can cry their eyes out?

"Aurora! You've got to get out of the street!" I yell.

But she just keeps crying.

"Aurora!" I yell again.

A new car starts beeping its horn.

I grit my teeth, heft Hector the Neglected higher onto my hip, and walk into the middle of the road.

But Aurora won't let me take her by the hand. "Up!" she says through her sobs, her arms raised up to me. "Up!"

So, I heave her up onto my opposite hip along with the diaper bag and—with all of those drivers watching impatiently —stagger across the rest of the road to where Bryce is still screaming and jumping about like his feet are on fire.

I quickly set Aurora and the diaper bag down on a snow-bank. "Don't you dare move," I say to her. "Not an inch!" My voice is shaking.

I turn back to rabid Bryce, flailing around on the shoulder of the road. I grab a rock off the ground with my Hector-free hand and close my fist around it. Then, I drop to my knees right next to Bryce and wrap him up with my arm. "Bryce, I have a rock for you that I need you to hold."

"AHHHH!!" he keeps screaming. "AH! AH! AH! AAAHHH!!" He keeps trying to squirrel out from under my arm, but I squeeze tighter.

"Bryce," I say again. "I have a rock for you that I need you to hold."

I glance at Aurora, and she's thankfully still sitting next to the diaper bag.

Bryce keeps squirming and keeps screaming, but it's weaker now than it was.

"Bryce, I have a rock for you that I need you to hold."

Bryce sinks against me. I open my hand so he can see the rock. He takes it in his right hand.

When things went south between my mom and Nate at the boat launch that day, I swear giving Bryce one rock after another was the only way I kept him with me. Sometimes you just need something solid that fits entirely in your hand.

I quickly grab another rock off the ground. "I have another rock that I need you to hold."

As he takes it in his other hand, the last bit of frenzy seems to leave him. He crawls up the black-tinged snowdrift to where Aurora is perched, curls up with his head in her little lap, and sobs.

I reposition Hector to be inside my jacket, zip it partly around him, and sit down next to Aurora and Bryce. I wrap the two of them up as best I can and give them kisses and kisses and more kisses.

Some people can do their homework. Some people get to have crushes on boys.

Some people have other things they've got to do.

CHAPTER 7

I look up when a car pulls up next to us.

Just please don't be that get-that-baby-a-coat guy. Can DCF take kids away from their big sister?

It's not him, but as soon as I see the driver's face I realize it's not much better. Because when you've just been humiliated and exposed as a totally incompetent person in front of a whole bunch of people, the next logical thing is to have your constantly-nagging-you-about-homework social studies teacher pull up next to you.

Ms. Rochambeau rolls down her window. "Zoey, I saw what just happened. Are you all okay?"

Bryce still has his face buried against my side, his chest heaving as I rub his back.

"Yeah, we're fine."

She eyes me. "Are you sure?"

I look down as Bryce wipes his nose on my jeans. "Yeah."

"I was hoping I could talk to you after class today, but you left before I had the chance," she says. "Did you really leave your packet at home?"

Is she kidding? She thinks I want to talk about homework right now? I manage to nod.

Aurora looks up. "Is she your teacher?" she asks between sniffles. "Does she give you graham qwackers and apple juice?"

Ms. Rochambeau doesn't take her eyes off me. "Is your packet really completed?"

"I told you it was. I was telling the truth."

"Bring it tomorrow. You can give your opening statement and then participate in the Q&A."

I freeze. Maybe I should have lied and said I hadn't done it.

At least I can always forget it a second time.

Ms. Rochambeau leans closer. "I want you to know that you remind me of me when I was your age."

I stare at her fancy turtleneck sweater and big jangly earrings. No way did she start out like me.

"And back then, there was one thing I needed more than anything else," she says.

"I told you. We're fine," I say.

Her eyes don't waver. "I needed to learn how to get people to take me seriously."

I stare at her. Every single day there's more and more proof that people will treat me how they treat me, and I don't have a shred of say in it.

"And I had to start with myself," she says. "Bring in that packet and don't sell yourself short."

She pulls into traffic before I can say anything in response.

If I do bring in my packet, it sure won't be because she told me to.

The only victory of the day is that somehow the power has come back on at home. Which is good timing because tonight is one of Lenny's guys' nights. I'm feeding the kids dinner in our bedroom because those guys get annoyed with us quick if we're out there with them, but I didn't get enough chicken nuggets on my first trip to the kitchen, so I pick up Hector and slip back out of the bedroom.

Lenny still has his jacket on because his second job at the nursing home goes until 6 p.m., but he's already holding a soda. "And then I've got this new young supervisor who's on my back all the time," he's saying. "You gotta wear these stupid plastic gloves—which makes sense most of the time because of how much disgusting stuff gets thrown out at old-fogey homes—but this new guy says we have to be wearing them ALL the time, and do you know how long it takes to get a trash bag open with those gloves on? And then he's telling me to pick up the pace? He doesn't have a clue." He takes a big swig of the soda, and then comes over to me and gestures for me to hand him Hector.

"How long have you been there now?" Slider asks as I pass Hector off.

"Four years next month. They hardly pay enough for it to be worth it, though. Talk about nasty." Lenny flies Hector up into the air to make him cackle a few times, and then hands him back to me.

With Hector back on my hip, I go into the kitchen and pull the freezer door open.

"Whatcha getting, Zoey?" Lenny calls.

"Just some more chicken nuggets for Bryce and Aurora." I grab the bag out of the freezer.

"You guys can never have enough, can you?" he says. "Just kidding. Here . . ." He starts coming over. "You won't be able to get the toaster to work without my help."

"That's okay." I pop the last four chicken nuggets into the toaster and jiggle the broken lever until it stays in the down position. "I got it."

"Because that toaster's fickle. It won't let just anyone get it to work."

"I know, but I—"

Lenny fiddles with the lever and finally gets it back to how I had it. "There," he says. "Your mother can't do it either."

I am not my mother, I think. But I don't say that out loud.

"Are you at the middle school?" one of the guys calls over.

"Yeah," I say. I try to make the "Yeah" come out like "Well, of course I am."

"Is that Ms. Rochambeau still there?"

At the mention of her name, I feel myself stiffen.

He leans over the back of the couch toward Slider. "Do you remember all that stuff we used to pull? Anything to try to make her cry."

"You were horrible," another guy says from his spot in front of the TV.

The first guy laughs. "What was I supposed to do? She called home when all I did was skip a detention. I got my beating, so she had to get hers."

"She's my social studies teacher," I say. I don't mention that she just pulled over on the side of the road to tell me to bring my homework to school.

"No way!" he says, slamming the back of the couch. "How is she still teaching? Do you remember those notes I hid all over her classroom that said, 'You're an ugly hag, and you'll die alone.'?" He's laughing so hard he can hardly talk. "She kept finding them for the rest of the school year!"

I keep my head down. I might not like her, but I wouldn't leave her horrible notes.

Out of the corner of my eye, I see Bryce come into the kitchen.

"Out of ketchup," he mumbles to me.

Lenny is at the fridge, pulling out another can of soda. Bryce silently hovers behind Lenny, waiting. But Bryce is so quiet that Lenny backs right into him as he shuts the fridge.

"Watch it, kid," Lenny says as he catches himself. Lenny never calls Bryce by his name. Says it's a sissy name. Somehow he thought the name Hector was way better.

Once Bryce recovers his footing, though, he just stands there not saying anything. It's like he's still on the side of the road watching Aurora about to get flattened.

Lenny looks closer at Bryce. "Your eyes look weird. You weren't crying earlier, were you?"

Bryce may be somewhere else, but he knows to shake his head "no" to that one. Knows that crying would be the worst thing in the world to admit to. But I'm pretty sure every single time he stops himself from crying, his nightmare factory just goes and creates another doozy for when he falls asleep.

"Well, don't you touch me," Lenny says. "I don't want to get whatever gross eye thing you got going on. And be a man about it. No complaining, okay?"

When Lenny leaves the kitchen, Bryce gets the ketchup out of the fridge, and I don't stop him when he brings the whole bottle back to the bedroom.

Bryce takes the two rocks to bed with him that night. At least when he wakes up from his nightmares, the rocks are right there for me to hand to him all over again. Lenny might be good for our family in general, but I'm not so sure he's good for Bryce.

CHAPTER 8

I put the debate packet in my backpack the next morning and have it with me when I get onto the bus—in part to get back at Lenny's friend for leaving those notes, but mostly because I want to.

Because I'm going to be top of my game today. I already managed to get Bryce and Aurora out the door on time, even though Bryce kept whacking things with his lightsaber every time I turned my back.

There's even a spot on the bus right close to the driver so I don't have to be anywhere near Kaylee and her nose. I sink into the seat and exhale.

When Matt Hubbard climbs up the stairs with his trumpet case, I peek to see if he looks at me. I can't tell, though.

He might have, but it also might have been a mistake, because usually someone else sits here.

Unfortunately, there are four hours between when I arrive at school and the Social Studies and Science Interdisciplinary Block. And even though I try to channel Silas's impenetrable wall, stuff finds its way in anyway. Side-looks at my clothes. Extra-long sighs from my teachers when I haven't done the homework.

And by the time I walk into social studies, I'm a mess. Just thinking about all those people looking at me while I'm up in front of the class has my hands doing their shaking thing.

Why? Why is this so scary? It's not running out of food. It's not losing our place to live. It's definitely not Aurora trapped in the middle of Route 3.

I try to take a deep breath. Around me, kids are going back and forth between the social studies and the science room where the wall usually is, and they don't seem nervous at all.

But I can't stop my hands from shaking, and when I take my packet out to put it on my desk, it's like a trembling white flag just trying to call attention to itself.

What if I do it without the packet? I know my octopus facts cold, right?

But as soon as I try to imagine what I would say, I can't remember anything. Everything has cleared out. It's like peering into an empty apartment the day after you've been evicted. The only thing there is a stray dirty sock that got left in the corner.

"All right, everyone," Ms. Rochambeau announces, while Mr. Peck settles down some kids at the back of the science room. "Today will mostly be focused on the second part of the debate: the question and answer period. Your goal is to get your fellow classmates to realize that your animal is better than the one they selected. A debate is always about getting someone to look at things in a new way."

Matt Hubbard raises his hand and asks something, but it's like I'm underwater, and not in an octopus sort of way.

I'm going to need the packet and I'll be worse than Calvin. I'm going to be a blubbering, shaking mess. Exactly who is going to change their mind about me based on that?

Exactly no one.

I stand up to sign out for the bathroom even though I was just there during English class. And on my way to the door, I do what I need to do.

I drop my packet in the trash can.

When I've finally gotten my hands to stop shaking and I come back to class, Ms. Rochambeau asks where it is.

But all it takes is a simple response.

"I forgot it."

Ms. Rochambeau's Raised Eyebrow of Disappointment only works if I'm looking at it.

I did the right thing, too, because when I take my seat again Holly Macnamore is trying to answer questions from Kaylee about giraffes, and it's not going well. Holly is nice. She went to the other elementary school and she and her friends let Fuchsia and me sit at their lunch table. We sit at two separate ends of the table, but still.

"Aren't they going to get neck issues when it's so long and skinny?" points out Kaylee. "And how can they hide from lions? Also, I don't see why—"

Ms. Rochambeau cuts her off before she can pile on any more.

Holly is all red and practically hyperventilating and both Nellie Abbott and Taylor Dixwell have their hands up like lions all ready for that giraffe.

"Remember to give the person you're asking the chance to answer one question at a time," says Ms. Rochambeau. "Holly, would you like to respond?"

Holly practically whispers. "Actually I think owls are better than giraffes anyway." And she sits back down.

Kaylee smirks and I can see her moving the points from the giraffe column to the owl column in her head.

I cross my arms and in *my* head I tally up all the many points that belong in the octopus column. Maybe no one else knows it, but I do.

I glance at Matt. And at least I didn't embarrass myself.

On the bus the next morning, Matt definitely doesn't look at me as he gets on, and he definitely doesn't look at me when he passes me in the hallway on his way to his locker. Maybe he caught sight of me once from his cozy spot on that tropical island of his, but he probably just decided it was the sun hitting a wave in a funny way. Or maybe a seagull.

Certainly not someone on the verge of drowning.

"What's wrong with you?" Fuchsia says, appearing at the locker next to mine.

I try to rearrange my face. "I'm fine," I say.

"Please," she rolls her eyes. "Spill it. What's up? Annoying grown-ups? Freaky nightmares? Boy drama?" She sucks in her breath. "You winced! That's it, isn't it?"

What is wrong with my face?

"There is no boy drama." No winces. No twitches. Especially because Fuchsia is the I-heard-that-boy-laughing-at-your-hair-so-I-punched-him-in-the-stomach-and-you're-welcome kind of friend. At least that's what she did in first grade. Before that we'd hung out because no one else wanted to be friends with us, but we were actual friends after the punching. Now she's less likely to actually punch someone since middle school punishments equal getting suspended and having to spend the day at home with her mom, but that's probably for the best.

"Sure there isn't." She nods. "Who is it?"

"No one."

"So, this no one likes you and you aren't interested? Or

this no one is older and gross and sending you perverted text messages?"

I stare at her. "I don't even have a phone."

She sighs. "So, it's the other way around then: you like him, and he won't give you the time of day."

"We should be talking about you," I say. "How's Jane Kitty?"

"Don't change the subject. Spill it. Who is it?"

She cocks her head, twirls a strand of pink hair, and stares me down. Like she'll be completely and thoroughly insulted if I don't tell her. But also like she might threaten to announce it to the world if I do.

I look away. When I had to move away during the spring of second grade, Fuchsia didn't talk to me for the whole week before I left. It didn't matter that she had moved plenty herself; her moves were always to somewhere else in town. What I was doing was unforgivable. When I moved back to town in fifth grade, she was cooler than before. Not actually cool, but more eye-roll-y and sigh-y and clothes-rip-y. She was still with one of her foster families then, and she claimed that she didn't care what they did or said, but when I saw the fifteen-year-old sister at after-school pickup one time, I realized that Fuchsia's hair had been dyed just like hers.

"I'm waiting!" she says.

The wall's bright white paint along the edges really helps the dark red brick stand out. If I were an octopus I'd be able to switch my skin to that exact brick pattern and blend right in.

"Fine," Fuchsia huffs. "Be that way." She walks away, and I'm left staring at a solid brick wall.

Matt isn't in homeroom for some reason, which helps make the case for the lack of boy drama. Maybe he's gone poof and suddenly stopped existing all together. That would solve a lot.

Unfortunately, Ms. Rochambeau hasn't gone poof because Mr. Bontaff drops a note on my desk.

> Zoey,
> Mr. Peck gave me the okay to switch your Wednesday Ace Period schedule. You'll no longer have extra help for science but instead will be required to attend the debate club I'm running in the library during that time. Bring a pen or pencil and a notebook. Also, next time you're throwing away your debate packet, you should use the paper recycling instead of the trash.
>
> See you soon,
> Ms. Rochambeau

Honestly? She went through the trash? Maybe she is more like me than I thought. But in what alternate universe do I belong in the debate club? I couldn't even handle standing up for two minutes to talk in class.

When Mr. Bontaff calls everyone to attention and announces that it's time for the student council election speeches, I stuff the note in my pocket. Maybe I'll be forced to go to her stupid debate club, but there's no way I'm participating. At least I have a say in that.

Our homeroom shuffles down to the multipurpose room, and as soon as I get there, I realize why Matt wasn't in homeroom: because he's running for seventh grade class president.

Up at the front of the room, the kids around Matt are fidgeting, but he's completely still, as though preparing to give a speech in front of a hundred-something kids is no big deal. If I had to stand up there at that podium, I'd probably blurt out "octopus" and pee myself.

Ms. Rochambeau is bustling about up in front, in charge of the whole thing. Of course. I wonder if she ever got married. I might not like her, but I hope she did just to show that friend of Lenny's.

As our homeroom sits down in its row, I see Amanda Dubois and Nicole Rochefort from Ace Period science extra help sitting together two rows in front of me. Even though I mostly spent the periods cleaning Mr. Peck's hermit crab tanks,

I liked the time with them. After they've finished doing their work, Amanda and Nicole can draw the best poodles, and they didn't mind that I'd peek over their shoulder. I wish there were kids like them on my bus or in my homeroom, kids that aren't all fancy-pants like Matt and aren't grimy like me and Fuchsia.

Meanwhile, in our homeroom row, fancy-pants Kaylee Vine and Nellie Abbott are making eyes at my shirt like it once mugged them in a dark alley. In my head, I spin my octopus funnel to point directly at them and dose them with a generous helping of freezing cold salt water.

I look around for Fuchsia, but she's in the alternative classroom, and they don't always come for grade level assemblies.

The speeches are boring. One girl talks for a long time about what kind of vending machine we should have in the cafeteria, but since you can't stick your free lunch ticket into a vending machine, I could care less about that.

When Matt stands up and walks to the podium I lean forward to see better. He has to be nervous. Are his hands shaking? How can they not be? How can he look so calm? There are so many people watching him. It's like he's not even human.

"Principal Fitzgerald, teachers, staff, my fellow classmates," he begins. "Thank you for this opportunity to speak. I'll keep it short, since I know there are more people that need to give speeches after me, and there's only so long you can listen to people talk about themselves."

He looks up from his piece of paper and smiles. A few

people around me giggle at his joke, and someone yells out, "Hubbard!" before a teacher hushes them—but all I can see is that smile. A real smile. Even when he was making a joke about himself. Like he knew everyone would get the joke because who doesn't think he should be standing up there? Like he couldn't even imagine someone calling him grimy or stupid or lazy or a troublemaker.

He goes on about how hard he works and how he'll work for the seventh grade so that we're represented in the way that we deserve. He says more stuff. And then he sits back down.

Other people stand up and talk, but I can't take my eyes off of Matt.

Because, suddenly, I know: This isn't some crush on a boy. This is me wanting to feel the way he does. Strong. Confident. Like no one would even *think* about messing with me.

Too bad that's even more impossible.

And just in case I needed the impossibleness of that to wave its giant hands in my face more directly, when I show up at the library for Ace Period debate club, guess who's sitting smack in the middle of one of the circular library tables like he owns the place?

Matt Hubbard.

CHAPTER 9

This would be a good time to turn around. I can still hide out in the bathroom all period if I need to.

"Zoey!"

I turn to see Mr. Herd, the librarian, standing on a chair next to a bulletin board for Martin Luther King Jr. Day, an open stapler in his hand. "Are you going to be doing debate for Ace Period? That's fabulous."

Right. Fabulous.

Ms. Rochambeau is coming toward me. "It's good to see you here. Do you have a pen and notebook with you?"

I nod. I don't say that I have no plans to actually use them.

She hands me a laptop. "Then, you've got everything you'll need."

I eye the other kids. They're all looking at Ms. Rochambeau

like eager beavers. I mean, there's no way I could ever be like them.

"Okay, everyone, find a seat," Ms. Rochambeau says. "Let's get started. And Mr. Hubbard, get off that table."

I slip into a chair at the table farthest away, but Ms. Rochambeau is having none of it. "Zoey, come sit up here." She motions to a chair next to a girl who must have gone to the other elementary school and who I think is in my English class.

All the kids go blurry when I make the switch from one chair to the other, but once I sit down they start to come back into focus. The girl does seem to be the same one who's in my English class, unless there are two brown-haired girls with a long braid and a habit of drawing cats all over their notebooks.

But more importantly, the other person at the table is Matt Hubbard.

Octopuses are supposed to smell like geraniums when they get stressed, and I'm pretty sure this whole library now smells like a bunch of geraniums exploded.

Ms. Rochambeau has dragged a rolling whiteboard over and holds a dry-erase marker over her head. "Now, you must always remember that the purpose of debate is to convince someone to see something in a new way."

I take a deep breath. I just have to stay calm. I've had plenty of practice blending in and doing nothing in all of my regular classes. And Ace Period only happens on Wednesdays. What's forty minutes once a week? I open my notebook, uncap my pen, rest my chin in my hand, and stare at a spot on the white-board just a bit to the side of Ms. Rochambeau's head. I've got this. I just have to keep my leg from going all jittery.

Ms. Rochambeau goes on about how a "resolution" is the statement in the debate that you're either arguing for or against, and other stuff, too, like about how if you're confident in what you say, people will take you more seriously. She says the word *confident* sixteen times in the space of five minutes.

I counted.

But one great thing about Ace Period debate is that every-one else likes to talk a whole lot, and none of the kids seem to care when I sit here totally mute. I manage to make it through the period unscathed. No embarrassment. No jittery leg. No total reveal of the mess I'd be if I had to stand up at a podium. And nothing for Ms. Rochambeau either. Because she might want me to jump through some silly hoop, but too bad.

Dolphins might jump through hoops, but I'm an octopus.

My mom doesn't have any hours at the restaurant today, and I find her at home sorting through the mountain of laundry while Hector takes clothes out of the pile and flings them around. Frank is watching one of his news programs and floss-ing his teeth.

"I'm going to walk to the laundromat," my mom says. "Lenny never has time to drive me, and this washing machine isn't about to start working again." She sighs and looks at the clothes still outside of the laundry basket. "But I can only take the important stuff. I can't carry it all."

I look at what's in the laundry basket. "Why is it just Lenny's stuff?"

She looks down like she hadn't noticed. "Well, you know how important it is to him to look put-together for work, and last night he was saying that he didn't have any clean pants to wear."

The pile of laundry already in the basket is pretty big, but I dig around in the leftover clothes until I find Aurora's pink sparkly leggings that desperately need to be washed. I hold them up for my mom to see. "Can these go in, too?"

My mom's eyes widen. "What happened to those knees?"

"Aurora was crawling around on the sidewalk, pretending to be Bryce's cat, and that's from the rock salt."

She laughs and deposits the leggings into the laundry basket. "She does make a good cat, doesn't she?"

I nod. "Her meow is so good I keep thinking there's an actual cat around."

"Maybe Bryce will stop asking for a real one," my mom jokes. "Because that sure isn't happening."

"Well, he hasn't brought it up in a while, so maybe." There's something about Bryce that's not-exactly-Bryce recently. He's stopped asking about a cat, and there was all that extra light-saber whacking this morning.

I eye the rest of the laundry. I want to add some of my clothes, but then I see Bryce's favorite Star Wars shirt that he spilled ketchup down the front of, and I grab that instead.

I hand it to my mom. Maybe getting his favorite shirt back will help him. "This, too?"

She eyes the plastic laundry basket that's now full to bursting and has a crack in the side, and I think she's about to say no, but she actually nods. And then in a move that's remarkably similar to old, competent mom, she retrieves some duct tape from a drawer and sits down next to the basket ready to do some reconstructive surgery. "You must have some of your clothes that you want washed, too," she says as she secures the tape around the plastic supports. "You should add a few things of your own."

"Really?"

She finishes her taping job and hefts the basket up to her hip. "Yeah, I think I can carry a bit more weight."

I look at her for a moment to see if she's kidding, but she doesn't seem to be, so I fish out a few shirts and a pair of jeans and toss them into the basket. Just like any good octopus, when there's an opening, I know to slip through it.

She looks at the clock on her phone. "It'll take me forty minutes to walk there, and then by the time I've gotten it all washed, I might as well wait for Lenny to get done with his shift and give me a ride home. It's right on his way, so he won't mind because it doesn't use extra gas, right?" She glances at the kitchen. "Can you cover dinner? I know these last few days of the month are tight. And Hector's been pretty fussy today. I think he's teething."

I watch as Hector chews on one of Aurora's shirts and then shrieks. I can tell where this is going: he's turning into one more screaming monkey. "I'll figure something out," I say.

My mom puts on her jacket and hoists the laundry basket onto her hip.

"Hey, Mom?"

She looks at me with her hand on the doorknob. "What?"

I picture Matt standing up at that podium making that joke.

"Do you ever feel . . . confident?"

"Confident?" She shakes her head as she pulls the door open. "The only confident I am is confident that life's never going to get any easier than this."

CHAPTER 10

But the next Sunday my mom doesn't have to work, and nei-
ther does Lenny. Lenny goes out to help a neighbor who is having some car issues, Frank is watching the Weather Channel,
and Bryce and Aurora are given the green light to pile into the
big bed with my mom and Hector for cozy time.

Alone in the kitchen, I fix myself a frozen waffle and eat it
looking out the window. All the trailers around us are gleam-
ing in the sunlight. It's one of those crisp, clear days that make
you think winter might not be all that bad.

After I brush my teeth, I peek in at them in my mom's bedroom. Hector is in the crook of my mom's arm, playing with
his toes, and Aurora is on her other side, her face buried in my
mom's T-shirt, like she can't breathe in enough of her smell.

Bryce has to be the lump that's under the covers down by my mom's knees.

My mom looks tired, but not as tired as usual. Like maybe Hector had one of his rare only-wake-up-twice nights.

She smiles at me. "It's an attack of the snuggle bugs."

Aurora burrows in deeper in response.

I sit down on the side of the bed near Hector and give his belly a tickle. It's his giggle button—and it almost always works. He lets out a happy cackle.

My mom nearly giggles, too. She's in a good mood today.

I decide to go for it.

"Can I take the bus down to the rec this morning?" I ask. "I promise to be back by two."

"No later than two?" My mom's brow furrows, but only slightly. She looks over to where the sunlight is shining around the corner of Lenny's nice curtains. Then, she nods. "Just don't miss the bus back. All my errands are on the other side of town this afternoon. I won't be able to pick you up."

I can't put my coat on fast enough.

Soon, I'm out in that sunshine, with bus money in my pocket, responsible for no one but myself for four whole hours.

Fuchsia is sitting on the steps just inside the rec, like I was hoping she might be. She smiles, her finger twisting around one of her bright pink side buns. "You came! You ready for your little plastic foosball men to get destroyed?"

I wait for her to start grilling me about the crush thing, but after multiple days of me insisting there's no such thing, I think she's finally started to believe me. She tosses me a folded-up white paper bag, and I sit down on the stairs next to her. I reach into the bag to find a giant glazed donut.

"It's a day old, but it takes a lot for a donut to go bad. Crystal brought home some almond tortes, too, but I know you don't like almond stuff."

"Thanks!" I say as I dig in.

Fuchsia's mom, Crystal, who Fuchsia unaffectionately calls by her first name, works the early shift at the bakery and currently has full custody of Fuchsia. But that happened only after Fuchsia got sent to foster care for a bunch of years. One rainy day back in second grade her mom was so strung out on drugs that she couldn't unlock the door to let Fuchsia into their apartment after school. Our teacher was still at school when soaked Fuchsia (then McKenna) turned up wanting to use the phone and the teacher asked questions and Fuchsia was too tired to lie. Supposedly, Fuchsia's mom has kicked the habit—at least she convinced the judge who gave her custody again that she had—but it's hard to know for sure. At least being able to bring home free baked goods is a perk.

When I finish eating my donut, I give Fuchsia's bright pink, Sharpie-covered sneakers a kick. "So, do you want me to remind you what happened the last time we played?"

She stands up. "You know your goals actually counted for negative points, so my score was way bigger than yours." She runs up the stairs before I can say anything in response.

Most of the kids who are at the rec on Sunday mornings play pickup basketball, so that means the game room is all ours. "I call red!" Fuchsia says, as I drop my coat on the pool table. "Those white guys were worthless last time I played you. When I tell them to block a shot, they're supposed to block that shot."

"It's not their fault." I stick a ball in and take a practice shot on goal with one of the white guys. "Their little plastic heads can barely believe my amazing skills."

"Wait, you can't start yet. I have to do my good luck dance first." Fuchsia closes her eyes and plants her feet on the ground like she's channeling supersonic powers from the blue-painted floorboards. She does finger-wiggling jazz hands and then moves into high knee lifts like in PE—with enough enthusiasm that I wonder if it's possible for her knee to smash into her nose. "Spinning skills get ready," she says. "Gonna spin it! Gonna win it!"

"Oh no," I say. "It's about being smooth." I slide my arms through the air like the tentacles they are and shimmy around the table. "No matter how small that opening is, I'll be slipping that ball right through it. It's called being a foosball boss."

"We'll see who the real foosball boss is." She rubs her hands together and then grabs the handles. "Spin to win."

Fuchsia proceeds to spin her handles like a maniac for the next five minutes, missing the ball nearly every time it passes by. She doesn't stop even when I score on her. "Spin to win!" she shouts over the thumpety-thump of the spinning plastic men as I collect the ball from her goal.

"How long do you think you can keep that up?" I ask.

"For forever. I promised Jane Kitty I'd score at least once the next time I played against you, so there's no time for slacking."

I load the ball back in. "Well, I hope Jane Kitty is ready to be disappointed because—"

Before I can finish my sentence, the ball rolls directly into Fuchsia's spinning offensive line just as their red bodies whip around. And with an earsplitting *smack*, they whack the ball straight into my goal.

"SKILLZ!" shouts Fuchsia.

She stops spinning her handles and switches into her victory dance, windmilling her arms as she leaps around the room.

I try to keep a straight face, but I burst out laughing. Especially because now she has grabbed a cue stick from the pool table and is wielding it like she's the very proud drum major in a very proud parade.

"I'm so glad you'll have good news to share with Jane Kitty."

Fuchsia whips her cue stick around until she's leaning on it like a cane. "Yeah, we should probably stop here. I think that was my good luck of the week."

So, we do. We move on to ping-pong and score based on who can hit the most surfaces around the room with a single shot.

CHAPTER 11

On the way to my bus stop on Wednesday I'm running my fingers through my hair because I didn't have time to brush it, when I see Silas coming down the steps of his trailer. Except his dad's truck isn't in the driveway like it usually is. "Where's your truck?"

Silas shakes his head and stares at the ground in front of him. "Still at the police station," he mumbles.

"What? Is everything okay?"

"Yeah, except that one of the teachers at school called the police when he saw our shotgun in the back of our truck when my dad was picking me up after school."

Silas is walking fast and I hustle to catch up to him. "What happened?" I ask.

"The police were nice enough. They got it that he was picking me up to go hunting. They just had to hold the truck overnight for 'security purposes,' but at least they gave us a ride to the woods around Squaretail Brook so we could go hunting, and my dad and I had a great time anyway. Still, that teacher wasn't a fan of hunting." Silas shakes his head. "If he eats meat he sure isn't thinking about where it comes from."

"You're going to keep hunting, though, right?"

"Of course I am."

I nod. "You better."

He looks at me for a long moment. "So, aren't you going to ask me what we found yesterday?"

I bite back a smile. "What'd you find?"

Silas stares up into the white sky. "More coyote tracks. Porcupine scat. And the newest snow was so dry that whenever some slid off a high tree branch, it was like shining bits of gold shimmering down in the sunlight."

I stare at Silas. I get why he keeps his mouth shut as soon as he's around other kids. Otherwise, people would stand in line just to beat him up.

"No signs of the bobcat?"

Silas grins. "Not yet."

On the bus, I ignore the eighth grade boy who pretend-coughs some comment I can't understand and lean my face against the window. I can see Matt's house as soon as we turn the corner onto his street. His front door is open, and when the bus pulls up in front of his house I can make out his mom in the door-way with him, pushing a travel mug into his hand. She gives him a kiss on the cheek just as he heads toward the bus.

"Is that coffee?" someone calls as Matt makes his way down the aisle of the bus.

"Yeah right," Matt says. "Banana peanut butter smoothie. I was up late working on that essay for social studies, and I didn't have time for breakfast."

I try to picture my mom pulling herself out of bed to make me a smoothie because I'm tired in the morning. As if she wasn't exhausted. As if she didn't have to take care of Hector. As if Frank wouldn't throw a fit for getting woken up by a blender. As if we had a working blender. As if we had bananas.

As if.

The seventh grade hallway is already jam-packed with bod-ies and backpacks when I arrive. As I make my way through the sea of shrieks and the rattle of lockers slamming shut, the slits of my octopus eyes stay horizontal. Octopuses have these little sacs called statocysts that respond to motion and gravity, so that their eyes can be totally unfazed, totally steady. It doesn't matter if the current whips all around and sends my tentacles off in some random direction, my eyes are always right side up. Never upside down.

Fuchsia is waiting for me at my locker wearing her black-painted jeans and shirt with intentional holes. When I get to my locker, she has her eyes closed as though she wasn't just watching me make my way through the hallway. She lets out a huge sigh.

"What's wrong?" I ask.

She opens one eye. "Oh, hey," she says. "When'd you get here?"

As though she wasn't just watching me. She's definitely not the Fuchsia who was dancing around the game room on Sunday. I start opening my locker.

She sighs again and rolls her eyes so slowly and dramatically that I wonder if her eyeballs are going to roll into the back of her head. She does not exactly have steady horizontal octopus eyes.

I give up. "What's wrong?" I ask again.

"It's all stupid."

I jiggle my locker open. "What is?"

I hang up my coat while I wait for an answer, but she doesn't say anything. I look at her and she's twisting up a flyer someone was handing out about some student council fundraiser. The top of it says something about buying Valentine's Day carnations for "Your Sweetie and Besties!" Mostly, though, she looks like she's going to throw up.

I push my locker shut. "What's going on?"

"Crystal and her goo brain decided we might be moving again."

"What?" I say. "To where?"

"Just down the street like we always do. I guess there's some guy, Michael, who's gonna cut us a better deal on rent, but ughh . . ." Fuchsia glares into my locker like it's Crystal's gooey brain. "I don't want to move again. *And* this Michael guy seems super sketch. He started hanging around Crystal at the bottle deposit a few weeks ago. Then, he offered to give her a ride to Walmart, and she let him. She had enough sense to not let him drive her home afterwards, but here we are three weeks later, and who cares if sketchy Michael doesn't know where we live because soon we're going to be moving into his very own sketchy apartment."

"Tell your mom you don't want to go."

Fuchsia shakes her head. "She waved some stupid custody paperwork in my face, and said I've got to do what she says." Fuchsia rips a piece off the flyer. "That's what she thinks."

Crystal can turn into a full-on defensive lineman when she wants to. Like when she and my mom had the big falling-out that ended their friendship, it was like Crystal tucked her head and tried to plow my mom right over. "Jealous," my mom said afterward. And, "That's why you don't poke your nose in other people's business." And Lenny added plenty of anti-Crystal words of his own.

Fuchsia turns around and kicks the locker she's been

leaning against. "*And* she doesn't think I'd be able to bring Jane Kitty with me because this Michael guy doesn't like cats."

I shut my locker. "What are you going to do?"

Fuchsia rips off another section of the flyer and starts balling it up between her fingers. "She said she'd call the cops on me if I refused."

I take a deep breath. "Are you sure this Michael isn't an okay guy? Have you seen him being sketchy?"

"I can tell. He's got sketch written all over him. Do *you* want to sign up to move in with him instead?"

"Maybe it won't be so bad," I say. "Maybe he'll fall in love with Jane Kitty just like you did. You could even get your own room."

"Yeah right." She glares at me like I'm the one forcing her to move. "I'll make sure you're the first to know when I do."

I try to keep my octopus eyes as steady as possible. "Well, what do you want me to—"

But Fuchsia cuts me off. "You know, maybe Crystal isn't the only one who can make a big deal phone call, because all I'd have to do is call that DCF person and start telling them stuff." Her eyes light up. "You know, I could tell her that. I could tell her that she's in for it if she goes ahead with this."

Several lockers down I hear laughter, and I turn to see a bunch of boys with Matt in the middle, telling some joke.

"And then if . . . " Fuchsia is saying. "Wait. What are you looking at?"

I quickly look away from the group of boys. "Nothing."

"Oh!" Fuchsia throws the little paper ball at me. "I was totally right, wasn't I? You *do* have some boy thing going on!"

"I do not."

"Say it then," she says.

"Say what?"

"Say: 'There is not a single boy in this hallway that I could be interested in.'"

"You're ridiculous." And too loud.

"Say it."

"You should get going to your homeroom," I say. "Aren't you going to get a detention if you're late again?"

"Say it."

I shake my head and walk away, past the boys—without looking at a single one of them.

"You didn't say it!" Fuchsia calls after me.

Fuchsia might have been the only girl willing to be friends with me when I moved back to town in fifth grade, but she doesn't always make it easy.

During this week's Ace Period, Ms. Rochambeau is going on and on about supporting your position with evidence. Too bad I'm pretty clear on my position already. It's: "I don't belong in

Ace Period debate club." And I've got plenty of "evidence" to back it up.

Evidence #1: Hermit crabs in the science classroom don't look down on me. The cat-drawing girl (whose name is apparently Lydia) is another story. I'm pretty sure she keeps shifting her notebook away from me. Matt hasn't even noticed I'm here.

Evidence #2: The hermit crabs need me because no one deserves to live in a filthy tank. And Lydia and Matt definitely don't need me.

Evidence #3: . . .

I stop when I realize Ms. Rochambeau is passing out worksheets. I sneak a peek at Lydia and then a super quick one at Matt. Both of them are already starting to read it. Hopefully, this can be like group work during regular classes where the other two people do the talking and my contribution is to not yell or throw up on anything.

And look. Twenty minutes later when it's the end of Ace Period, my worksheet is throw up–free. Victory is mine! And I don't care that Ms. Rochambeau raises her eyebrows when she picks up my worksheet and it's blank. I'm here, aren't I? No one can force me to do more than that.

Two periods later is social studies, and Ms. Rochambeau is coming around to collect an essay that's due—that I've yet again done a wonderful job of not doing.

"Zoey," she whispers when she gets to my desk and I don't have anything to turn in. "I'd like you to stay after class, so we can talk."

I don't say a word or even nod, but she walks away like I've agreed to it. Sure enough, when there's just a few minutes left of class and my tentacles start working to gather up my papers, Ms. Rochambeau, who has been reading us excerpts from Daniel Webster's, Henry Clay's, and John Calhoun's speeches in Congress about the Compromise of 1850, wanders over to my desk without missing a beat and rests her hand on my notebook.

It doesn't matter how many tentacles I have. She's not going to let me pack up my notebook.

When the class has been dismissed and I'm still in my seat, Ms. Rochambeau finally removes her hand from my desk.

"Thank you for staying after, Zoey," she says.

I didn't exactly have a choice.

Ms. Rochambeau pulls the neighboring student desk over and sits down in it. "Now," she says, her big earrings bouncing off the collar of a different turtleneck sweater, "we could talk about how much your grade will suffer if you don't turn in this reflection essay, but instead I want to talk about something else. I want to talk about your participation in debate club."

I watch her through the slits of my octopus eyes. Nice and steady.

"I want to know why you're not trying."

I glance at the clock.

"And I want to know what kind of person you want to be."

I want to be the kind of person that doesn't have to sit here and have this conversation.

"What's your next class?" she asks.

"Computer tech," I say. "So it's all the way down in the other wing." So I'd better leave right now.

"Great," she says without standing up. "That means we have the next forty-three minutes to dig into this. I have a prep period right now, and Mr. Roberts will definitely understand why you weren't able to be in class today—I'll be happy to talk to him about it over lunch."

It's like my octopus body has gotten trapped in a net. But there has to be an opening somewhere. If I can just stay calm and avoid getting tangled up . . .

"Marcy?" Another teacher pops her head into the room. "Do you have a minute?"

It's my opening. My tentacles spring back to life, and I stand up from my chair.

"Sit back down," Ms. Rochambeau says to me. To the other teacher she says, "Sorry, another time maybe? This is important."

I slide back into my chair. In a net—and now I'm getting poked with a stick.

She even thinks it's important to poke me with a stick.

Important.

Me.

Once the other teacher is gone, Ms. Rochambeau turns back to me. She says things, but I'm not listening. No one has ever connected *me* with being important. The things that they want me to *do* are important—do my homework, bring a pencil, wear sneakers for PE.

But this somehow feels different.

Ms. Rochambeau has stopped talking and is looking like she's waiting for me to say something.

When I don't, she says again, "Zoey, what kind of person do you want to be?"

I stare down at my notebook. What am I supposed to say to that?

"I don't know," I finally mumble.

I wait for Ms. Rochambeau to say that's okay—because "I don't know" almost always gets a teacher to move on—but she doesn't. Instead she stares at me harder and finally says, "Then, I'm glad you have some time right now to think about it."

I shift in my seat.

"Here," she says, "stand up. I want you to come over here." She goes over to her desk in the front corner of the room and starts clearing off the top of it. She moves a pile of paper to the top of a filing cabinet, and then pulls out the cushy rolling chair. "Come sit," she says.

"At your desk?"

She nods. "I want you to imagine you're an adult. And I want you to picture the life you want to have. Oh, and hold on . . . " She bends down and rummages in one of the cupboards behind her desk until she pulls out a bag of pretzels. "Good hard thinking is always a lot easier with food."

I slowly make my way toward her desk. When I finally reach the cushy, rolling chair, I look at her. "Really?"

"Really," she says.

I sink down into it. I rest my arms on its armrests. I lean my head back. I survey the classroom like a kingdom. Like all those hard plastic desks are *my* kingdom.

I lean forward and take a pretzel.

I'm ready to start telling myself a story about the pretzel-eating queen when Ms. Rochambeau takes a seat in the front row of student desks.

"Does it feel different there?" she asks.

I nod. I take another pretzel.

"Good," she says. "That should help. Sometimes the walls of the hole we're in are too close for us to see anything else."

I stop eating the pretzel. "Are you saying I'm in a hole?"

Ms. Rochambeau doesn't move. "Do you think you're in a hole?"

I feel my brow furrowing against my will. I need to be an expressionless wall that things just bounce off of, like Silas. Or even better—so slimy that things slide right off, like any good octopus.

Because if people see that they're getting to you, they'll never let up.

"Of course not," I say quickly. I try to pretend that things are so easy right now that I could never even consider my life as a hole. Because it's like beautiful, flat, easy-walking ground, all the time now, right? Maybe some bumps along the way, but that's just like the beautiful rolling hills they show on the ads to remind people that they should come to Vermont for vacation.

"You know that the Ace Period debate club is ending, and a new rotation starts next week, right?"

Do I know that? Of course I don't. But since I don't usually listen to the teacher, that makes sense.

Ms. Rochambeau leans forward. "The real debate club is going to be starting after school next week, and I want you to be part of it."

"Because I've done such a great job during Ace Period?" The crack slips out before I can stop it, but Ms. Rochambeau doesn't flinch.

She just keeps staring me down.

She can't be serious. "But after school I need to—"

"Pick up your brother and sister, right?" she says. "What time does the Head Start bus drop them off?"

"Umm . . . about 3:55?"

"Great. Debate club goes until 3:30, and then I can give you a ride right to their bus stop. I've checked to make sure that I could legally drive a student, and as long as your mom gives consent, it's fine."

She'd be willing to be my personal driver? It's mind-blowing enough that I can almost forget that we're talking about staying after school for debate club.

Almost, but not quite.

"We'll meet every day after school except for Tuesday when there's a faculty meeting. The tournament is at the beginning of March." She gives me a hard look.

I look away.

"Zoey, only you can choose what kind of person you become."

My eyes drift to the tops of the trees I can see out the window. Bare branches. Gray sky. Nothing else.

"That assumes I have a choice," I say.

Ms. Rochambeau practically leaps out of her seat. "But you *do* have a choice. You make choices every day, and maybe you can't see how they could affect your future, but they do."

She is quiet for a moment as she stands there. "I want you to know," she finally continues, "that I was the first person in my family to graduate high school and go to college. Since life isn't fair, it's often up to us to balance it out."

I look at her. She's looking back at me like she's trying to explode me with her eyes. "What made the difference for me," she says, "was the advice someone gave to me back when I was in middle school."

I still don't believe she was like me.

"It wasn't fair, and it wasn't easy," she continues. "But it was the only way forward if I wanted a future for myself."

I want to look away, but I also want to know what they said. "What was it?"

She chews on her lip without taking her eyes off me. "I'll tell it to you, and then I'm going to leave you alone for the rest of the period."

"Okay."

"Are you ready?" she asks.

I nod.

"You sure?"

I nod again.

"Well here it is . . . " She stands up. "Suck it up."

Then she picks up a folder of papers and walks out of the room.

CHAPTER 12

I'm so angry that I don't hear a single thing anyone says for the rest of the day. How could a teacher have the nerve to say something like that? How? What does she think I've been doing my whole life? All I want to do is write mean notes to leave around Ms. Rochambeau's classroom. And the "Ms." is probably an unmarried "Ms." because no one would marry a miserable person like that. I glare out the bus window as we pull out of the school parking lot. Stupid school. Stupid teachers. They think they're so smart.

They don't know anything.

But whatever. Even when the oxygen level in water drops, an octopus can still manage to maintain a constant intake of oxygen. Can still find a way to keep breathing.

When the bus stops to let off the kids who live in the neighbor-hood near the hospital, I glance over at Silas. He's tucked into the corner of his seat, his knees up to his chest and his camo trucker hat pulled down so low that I can't tell if he can see. Silas, who has had plenty of kids trying to make his life miserable.

Suddenly, I feel bad about wishing all those nasty notes on Ms. Rochambeau. Still, if I told Silas about all the stuff that I have to deal with, would he tell me to suck it up?

"Silas?" I say.

Nothing. No response. No words. No twitches.

Maybe he didn't hear me. "Silas," I call louder.

He's like a vault of silence. He has perfected the expres-sionless wall.

I'd bet anything he's never answered a single question in class.

When we get off the bus and the other kids from the bus stop have spread in other directions, I look over at Silas again, and this time he looks back.

"Hey," I say.

"Hey," he says. All normal, like his on/off switch has been flipped and, of course, he can talk now.

"Why do people say stupid stuff?" I blurt out. "Like stupid, I-know-better-than-you-and-you're-just-a-waste kind of stuff."

Silas doesn't answer. He's still walking alongside me, but his face has changed. Like it's gone back to an emotionless wall that isn't going to let anything in or out.

"Silas?" I say.

"I don't know," he whispers. Then, he peels off, heads up the couple steps to his trailer, and disappears inside.

At least that was better than "Suck it up."

As soon as I walk into the trailer, I remember. Today is the first of the month, which means a refilled EBT card, which means:

A stocked fridge.

Cabinets with cereal.

A new full bag of chicken nuggets in the freezer.

I go straight over to the fridge to examine its contents. Milk. Juice. Eggs. Yogurt. One package of uncooked chicken and a package of ground beef. I grab a coffee yogurt, shut the fridge, and dig in the drawer for a spoon.

I take my first bite of yogurt and it melts in my mouth like ice cream. It's like my old competent mom is back, and that mom knows I love coffee yogurt.

Because when someone is doing the best they can, you don't tell them to suck it up. The right thing to do is buy them coffee yogurt.

The walk to the Pizza Pit today isn't too bad because it's not windy, but the side of the road has enough puddles of semi-frozen slush that my feet are cold and wet by the time I get there.

My mom is sitting at a booth with Hector in her lap, folding cardboard pizza boxes.

"Thanks for the coffee yogurt," I say as I reach for Hector. I slip my feet out of my sneakers and tuck them up underneath me as I slide into the seat across from her.

My mom looks up from her folding and almost smiles. "It's a good day."

Hector grabs onto my cheek, and it hurts, but he's so pleased about it that I let him. "Did you go to the grocery store today?" I ask him. "Did you get to ride in a cart?"

"Walmart, not the grocery store," my mom says. There's a spark in her eyes, the old-mom kind of spark. "Like that bag of chicken nuggets was two dollars cheaper than anything they have at the grocery store. And then with all the savings I was able to make another payment on the phone bill, and that gets us closer to getting out from under that ridiculous interest rate."

"How'd you get all the way to Walmart?"

She leans forward. "Well, I found out that the bus that goes by the Cumberland Farms in the morning now has a stop at the train station, so then all Hector and I had to do after that was walk over the bridge into New Hampshire and up that hill to get there." She puts another folded box on the pile. "And then Lenny picked us up to bring us back home in the break between his jobs."

"Did you get more diapers?"

She nods. "Just a small package this time so I could make that phone bill payment. But I feel it, Zoey. I feel like things are going to get better. I know you've been working so hard, and I'm hoping that at least I'll be able to clean your clothes for you more often. We're so close to being able to start saving for a functioning washing machine."

It's like she's my old mom again. The old mom who would zero in on a project like a laser. The old mom who told jokes. The old mom who would climb into her car and step on the accelerator like she meant it.

The bell jingles and an elderly man walks through the door. My mom hops up and grabs a menu. "A table for one, sir?" she says. "Right this way please."

At one of the restaurants my mom used to work at (before her teeth got bad), it was fancy enough to have a hostess separate from the waitstaff, but I kind of like it smaller like this. It feels more like a home.

Connor pushes through the kitchen doors, wiping his hands on his apron as he goes. He slows down and his face breaks into a smile as soon as he sees me with Hector and realizes my mom's already been able to greet the customer.

"My fabulous Zoey!" he says, sitting down where my mom had been. "How was your day?"

"It was okay." The coffee yogurt and getting a glimpse of old mom made up for a lot.

"Hold on," he says.

A moment later, he comes back with an ice water that has a nice fat lemon slice perched on the rim. "Now. Do you want to talk about it?" Connor leans back and pushes up his sleeves. I can see his tattoos better now. That two-way cross with all these designs around it.

"What's the story behind that tattoo?" I say, pointing. "That one that's like a cross? You got that in Peru, right?"

"This one?" Connor says, pushing his sleeve up higher to reveal all of it. "I was in Cusco, and I'd been backpacking for weeks." He traces his finger around its edges. "I was still so raw from the fallout after coming out to my parents, and I was starting to worry that I was only there because I was running away."

Hector squirms and I shift him up higher on my lap, trying to keep him quiet so Connor will keep talking.

"But it was still good to be there. I don't think it's healthy to always stay in a place like this where almost everybody is white like us. This was a place filled with all kinds of people; it's a place where brown people were once kings." He taps his tattoo. "And I kept seeing this symbol all over. My Spanish wasn't great and I didn't know any of the native Quechua, but

I finally got up my courage and did my best to ask a woman selling souvenirs what it meant."

Hector keeps squirming and I spread out the Sweet'N Low packets on the table for him to play with.

"She said it's called the *chakana* and that there are different interpretations of its meaning," Connor says, leaning forward. "What she believed, though, was that it represents the state in which all beings are their complete selves. And that the empty space in the middle of the cross was a portal for people to enter and fully understand how we're all children of the stars. That was the moment." He looks out the window and smiles. "I wasn't running away anymore. I had run *to* what I needed to find."

Hector knocks a bunch of Sweet'N Low packets onto the floor, but I ignore it.

"I hadn't ever considered getting a tattoo before, but I had this on my arm by the time I fell asleep that night." Connor brings his arm up and gives the tattoo a kiss. "Sometimes life gives you a moment like that where everything is suddenly clear. And for me, it's good to have a daily reminder of it."

A moment when everything is suddenly clear.

Like when you start to wonder if maybe you do have a choice about the kind of person you want to become.

Maybe.

CHAPTER 13

It's after 11 p.m. when my mom gets home from work. I'm lying in bed—mostly because the TV show that Frank had been watching is the one with the news guy that's angrier than all other news guys and who makes me feel like the whole country is just minutes away from exploding. Lenny is in his bedroom and is probably organizing my mom's clothes for her. Still I don't feel like going to sleep, and when I hear my mom get home I tiptoe past Bryce and Aurora and push open the door into the main room.

I don't see my mom, though. Frank is still watching that show—this time it's a secret government drone conspiracy that's going to make everything go up in flames—and he doesn't even notice me. I cross the room to see if she's around the corner in the entryway. Her coat is there, tossed on the washing machine, but no Mom.

Then, I hear her voice through the wall. She's already in the bedroom with Lenny. I peek back around the corner at Frank—he's still soaking up this drone conspiracy like a rebel army might show up at our door, asking him to join up, but he'd need to have memorized all of the details from this show to ride off into the sunset with them.

He has definitely not noticed me.

I slip back behind the corner and climb up onto the washing machine next to my mom's coat. Then, with my unblinking octopus eye, I peer through that little lightsaber hole.

My mom, still wearing her Pizza Pit uniform, hasn't gotten very far into the room. She's frozen, watching Lenny. Lenny is organizing his drawer of undershirts (maybe he's already done with her shirts), and he's keeping his voice low. That's probably so he doesn't wake up Hector who's asleep in the crib in the corner, but there's something about him that's kind of twitchy.

And then I make out what he's talking about: yogurt.

"You could get a pound of ground beef for the price of two of those yogurts. And they're so small. I ate one and it was gone in three bites."

"I know," my mom whispers, "but they're healthy, and the kids love those yogurts."

"So you're saying I'm some horrible kid-hating person just because I don't like them? You're always trying to make things into an argument." He unfolds the shirt and starts folding it from the beginning again.

She didn't say he hated us, did she? Isn't she just being the competent kind of mom who gets her kids yogurt?

"I didn't mean it like that. It's just that I want to be able to—"

"You want to be able to tell the kids that it's my fault that they have to eat hamburgers instead of that stupid yogurt. Fine, go ahead. Go wake them up. I bet they'll thank me."

His voice. I didn't know a quiet voice could be that piercing.

My mom doesn't say anything. Her head is down, and when I look closer I realize she's crying.

"Oh, poor baby," Lenny is saying. "Turn on the waterworks to see if that'll help. But sorry, you're not going to manipulate me that way."

And suddenly I realize, it doesn't matter what she actually says to him. He's not going to take any part of it seriously. My old mom was confident before, but it wasn't enough. Her confidence has been sucked out of her, and she's been left bone dry.

My mom still doesn't say anything in response. Her chest is heaving, but she's not making a sound.

Lenny walks over to my mom like he's going to console her. He stops right next to her, his nose practically in her ear. "If you didn't have me to take care of you, you'd be out on the street. And no one cares about a chick on the street."

My mom is trying to get hold of her breathing. Like she's trying to say something.

"Oh, spare me the drama. You always have to have the last word, don't you?" Lenny snaps. "Well, sorry. I'm not going to stick around for it. You're such a joke."

His words ring in my ears, but all I can see is my mom hunched over, trying desperately to calm down enough to say something.

When she finally manages to, it comes out in a whisper. "I know."

Somewhere inside of me I feel something crumble. Those two whispered words are too much for me.

But just then, Lenny heads for the door right next to where I'm sitting on the washing machine.

He can't see me here. I curl up closer to the wall, but there's hardly any need. He shoots out of the bedroom like it's a cannon, and a second later he's already at the fridge.

Quickly, I slip off the washing machine, and when his head is stuck in the fridge I dart back across the room.

He stands up just as I reach my bedroom door.

"What are *you* doing up?" he snaps.

It's like his voice from back in the bedroom is still kicking around.

"Had to go to the bathroom," I mumble. I quickly slide into the dark bedroom and close the door behind me.

When I get into my room, I curl up on my mattress and

shut my eyes tight. Maybe I can just go to sleep. Maybe I can pretend that everything's fine.

Except that I know where my old mom went now.

Lenny stuffed her into a box and locked it tight.

I stare at the glow of the Mickey Mouse night-light. It's been with us in all the gross apartments. It was even there in the months I'd like to forget when there was no apartment and all our stuff was in the back of a car.

Lenny was supposed to make everything better.

Because I was so sure that the most important thing was having a good, stable place to stay.

I try to breathe. In. Out. Come on—even when the oxygen levels drop, octopuses can still do it. In. Out.

I push up onto my fists and reach through the pile of stuff on the floor between my mattress and the wall. Finally, I pull out a black Sharpie. In the glow of the Mickey Mouse night-light I make my way across the room and slip behind the curtain to stand against the window, where the glow is coming instead from the next door neighbor's porch light. And, there, I tug my shirt aside to reveal my shoulder, and I start drawing.

My very own octopus tattoo. With strong tentacles lined with suckers and an unblinking eye that stares everyone else down.

Because this is my moment when everything is suddenly clear.

I'm not going to be like my mom. I'm not going to let anybody mess with me.

When an octopus sends up its spray of ink, it means business. It's going to throw off that predator—and then it's going to escape.

And nobody's a better escape artist than an octopus.

CHAPTER 14

When I get to the Pizza Pit on Thursday afternoon, Hector is being held by Connor and getting cooed at by a table of old ladies. Even though I'm here on a mission, it seems wrong to take Hector away from them, so I take a seat at the usual employee table and listen as they call him Mr. Handsome Pants and he squeals in happiness. When Connor finally brings Hector over to where I'm sitting, the old ladies are still playing peekaboo with him over Connor's shoulder.

"When did you get here?" Connor asks as he slides in across from me. "Did the bell on the door even ring? I must be losing the hosting touch if I missed that completely."

Connor hands Hector to me as Hector lets out a cackle of glee. I glance over at the old ladies and see one of them reappearing from behind a napkin. I bite back a smile, and turn to Connor. "You were pretty well occupied."

"Alright, so what do you think?" Connor says. "You're in Siberia by yourself, but you can listen to all of your favorite music, or you're in a mosh pit at a concert where they keep playing your most hated song over and over again."

"Easy," I say. "Siberia."

"What if it's for ten years?"

"Still easy," I say. "We're talking about the 'Barbie Girl' song that plays every time Lenny gets to the part in his video game where the booby lady comes out. Nothing would get me to choose the mosh pit."

Connor surveys me with his finger to his lip like he now has to send all of his mosh pit extras home. "Fair enough."

I glance toward the kitchen doors. "What's my mom doing?"

"She decided we needed to do an extra scrub down of the bay where we make the salads, so she's tackling that."

"Do you know what her work schedule is like for next week?" I ask.

Connor nods. "Same as mine. Monday, Tuesday, Wednesday, Thursday, Saturday."

I exhale. *How am I going to make this work?*

"What's up?" Connor says. "What are you thinking about?"

I shake my head. "It's stupid."

Connor leans forward and points his finger at me until

it almost touches my nose. "You're not stupid, so whatever you're thinking about can't be stupid. Now tell me."

I open my mouth but then close it again. Did I really think the after-school debate club could be my ticket out? How am I going to be an escape artist octopus if I can't even say it out loud? I take a deep breath. "It was this after-school activity."

"And if your mom's at work you can't do it?"

"There's a teacher at school who will drive me to Bryce and Aurora's bus stop, but that doesn't help me pick up Hector."

"But that's just fifteen minutes."

"It's twenty or twenty-five minutes if you count the time it takes me to get Bryce and Aurora off the bus and walk back here with them."

"Okay, so it's twenty-five minutes," Connor says. "Still."

I shake my head. "Well, it's not like Ricky's going to let my mom move her whole shift back twenty-five minutes. Just for some stupid after-school activity."

"No," Connor says, "but I could watch Hector until you get here—for free," he adds.

"But why would you—"

"Because the more you call this after-school activity stupid, the more I think it's required for you to do it. What days does it meet?"

I study the shaker of red pepper flakes. "Every day except Tuesday," I say. "The teacher is kind of intense."

I glance up to see him smiling. "That's the best kind of teacher."

My mom pushes through the kitchen doors, wiping her hands on her apron.

"Good news," Connor says. "We've figured out a way for Zoey to do an after-school activity that she needs to do."

My mom cocks her head. "How . . ."

Connor jumps in. "I'm going to get to play with Hector until Zoey can get here."

My mom looks between us a few times like she's trying to figure out what the trick is.

I take a deep breath. "I just need you to give permission for my social studies teacher to give me a ride to Bryce and Aurora's bus stop when it's over. I'll be able to pick them up just like normal."

She peers at me. "So, there are people bending over backwards to make this happen?"

"Yeah, I don't know why." I glance at Connor. "It's just an after-school activity."

My mom shrugs. "Well, if you want to do that, it's fine with me. Nothing's going to change too much." She looks at Connor. "Are you sure? You know we can't pay you."

Connor smiles wide. "Couldn't be more sure! And now. . . ." He smacks the table as his eyes light up. "It's all set." He leans closer and whispers, "Look out, you stupid after-school activity. Here comes Zoey!"

"Connor," my mom says. "It looks like your table is ready to pay. Do you want me to take care of it?"

Connor shakes his head. "I got it." Then, he looks at me. "When does this all start?"

I bite my lip. "Monday."

"Great," he says.

Great, I think. Like: Isn't it *great* I just signed up to voluntarily gnaw my own arm off?

My mom sits down where Connor was before and starts rolling silverware into napkins. The wrinkles across her forehead are deeper than they used to be.

"Thanks for buying us yogurt," I blurt out.

"What?" she says, startled. "Oh yeah, that."

"It's really good," I say. "And it's healthy, too. My teacher for health class loves to talk about how good yogurt is for you."

My mom nods absently.

"My teacher also says that it's not good to eat too much red meat."

My mom's eyes slowly work over to me. "I don't know what you're talking about."

"I'm just saying that if you want to buy yogurt, no one should be allowed to stop you."

My mom's eyes narrow into a full-on glare, her jaw tight. She grabs the finished silverware rolls and stands up—without a word—and walks off. A moment later, the kitchen doors swing shut behind her, and she's gone.

She's never going to step into a dairy aisle again, is she?
Mom thinks that nothing's going to change too much.
It's up to me to prove her wrong.

CHAPTER 15

The next day at the end of social studies class, it's me who is lingering. When Ms. Rochambeau finishes up a conversation with one of the girls who's obsessed with getting a 100, I step forward. "My mom said it's fine if you drive me, but . . ."

"But what?" She puts down the stack of rubrics she's holding.

"Are you sure you can do it?"

"Absolutely," Ms. Rochambeau says. "It'll be my pleasure."

I look down at the floor. "Because if I don't get on the bus, and then for some reason you can't . . ."

She puts her hand on my shoulder. "I will be just as reliable as a bus. I promise."

And the final excuse flies out the window.

On Monday when the dismissal bell rings, convincing my feet to walk to the library feels impossible. Those other kids are going to know that I'm choosing to be there. That I think I deserve to be there.

When I get to the window that overlooks the parking lot, I pause. The buses are still at the curb, idling their engines. If I make a break for it now, I could skip out on this and ride the bus home like normal.

On the other side of the pickup area, I spot Fuchsia leaning against a NO PARKING sign, fiddling with her phone. It's just for show, though, because I know she doesn't have any minutes. Not that she could tell me that in a normal way. She had to sigh seven times and roll her eyes thirteen different directions just to get me to ask the right question about it. Lately it seems like I'm just a warm body whose job is to play her eye-rolling games. I move the collar of my camo jacket aside and reach under my shirt to touch my octopus tattoo. An octopus would get taken seriously.

If I looked like one of the eager beaver kids from debate, everything would be different. I close my eyes. I can camouflage myself well enough to blend in with a desk. I just need to camouflage myself enough to blend in with them.

I take a deep breath and flex my tentacles. Then, I head for the library.

By the time I get there, Ms. Rochambeau has already started the meeting. "Now the first thing that makes this different from Ace Period debate club is the tournament that's at the end," she's saying.

I slip into the same chair where I sat for Ace Period and produce my notebook and pen like all the other kids around me.

"It's a statewide tournament with students from all over Vermont, so I want to make sure you're as well prepared as possible. We'll start by digging into skills and techniques, and then zero in on preparing a specific debate topic after that. One of the debates at the tournament will be the topic we've prepared—but you don't know which side you'll get assigned. The other one will have a topic that gets assigned by the judges, so you have to be ready for anything. Our goal this month is to make you the confident debaters you need to be for the tournament."

I block out most of the stuff about the tournament that there's absolutely no way I'm going to. But I do make note of another *confident* for Ms. Rochambeau's general tally. (She's up to twenty-eight.) I can still blend in with the eager beavers. I can still pretend I'm like them. Maybe after long enough, that magic wand of confidence will mistake me for them, and give me a bop on the head, too.

"Now, today we'll be discussing your most important defensive tactic . . . " Ms. Rochambeau starts writing on the board.

From behind me, a boy calls out before she's even written two letters down. "Discrediting your opponent!"

"Exactly." Ms. Rochambeau finishes writing it, underlines it, and then wanders over close to my table. I squish my boneless octopus body down to its small-bag-of-chips size.

"To discredit someone means to undermine them," she says. "But there's an important distinction you all need to pay close attention to. You are not trying to undermine your opponent as a person. You are simply trying to undermine their argument. Who can give me an example of what that means?"

One of the eighth grade boys jumps out of his seat. "Like if someone is using research to show that schools should get rid of homework, you could point out that they probably did that research at home and that they've proven your point for you."

Ms. Rochambeau tilts her head. "Sort of like that. Can someone give us another example?"

A black girl who's sitting at the other eighth grade table raises her hand, and Ms. Rochambeau nods to her. "Go ahead, Kyla."

"It's like if someone was arguing we shouldn't have affirmative action in colleges because it's an unfair advantage," Kyla says, "and then I point out that the real unfair part is the four hundred years of systematic oppression that made it harder for

African Americans to go to good schools and get good jobs just because of the color of their skin."

Lydia shifts in her seat like the words themselves are making her uncomfortable. Maybe if I knew what affirmative action was I'd feel uncomfortable, too. Maybe if I thought that there was even a chance of me going to college.

"Exactly," Ms. Rochambeau is saying. "Now, who can give an example of something that would be a personal attack, of what you shouldn't do?"

Matt raises his hand. "If we were talking about the dress code, it wouldn't be appropriate if I told Lydia that she can't be objective about it since she's a girl and girls are obsessed with how they look."

Matt has hardly finished speaking when Lydia whacks him on the head. Not in a flirty way either. In a don't-you-even-dare way.

"Right," Ms. Rochambeau says, ignoring the whack. "We respectfully point out the holes in an opponent's argument, but we don't attack the person themselves. It's their argument that isn't as good as yours, not them. Keep it separate."

That's funny. Since when does the world work like that?

"Now, there are several different ways to approach it," Ms. Rochambeau is saying. "First, you can show that your opponent's point is insignificant compared to your point, just like Kyla's example."

I glance back at Kyla, and she's taking notes on everything

Ms. Rochambeau is saying, maybe word for word. She means business.

"Second," Ms. Rochambeau continues, "you can prove your opponent's point isn't relevant, or third, you can turn their point around and show how it actually proves your side instead." Ms. Rochambeau picks up a stack of papers and starts passing them out to each table. "In your table groups, you're going to be picking out examples from a debate that's transcribed here. Identify instances where one of the participants attempted to discredit the other, and then look for any missed opportunities."

I glance at Matt and Lydia and pick up the paper just like they do. I start reading it, but keep sneaking peeks at them to make sure I'm still on track. When they start shifting around like they're done reading, I still have one more paragraph to go—probably because of all that peeking—so I skip it and pretend I'm done too even though I actually really want to finish. The "resolution" for the sample debate was that "Fair governments should require employers to pay a living wage," and I kind of have an opinion on that. Like I keep waiting for the paper to talk about how amazing it'd feel if your family didn't need to fill out that government form for an EBT card. And if you had enough money to buy new underwear as soon as you need it.

Lydia is the first one to talk. "So, what if we highlight all the examples?"

"Sure," Matt says, "that sounds good."

"Do either of you guys need a highlighter?" Lydia asks, digging into her bag. "I've got a ton of them." She fishes out a handful and deposits them in the middle of the table.

"Thanks." Matt takes a blue one.

She really meant me, right? I glance up. She's looking at me like she did. This whole blending in like an eager beaver is working better than I thought. "Thanks," I murmur. I reach out and slide the closest highlighter toward me.

"Okay, so that first line in the second paragraph is definitely one," Matt says. "Where Debater #1 says it doesn't matter if someone's wage goes up if they get fired, and they'll get fired because the company can't afford to pay them more. That's showing their point is more important than the other person's point. And probably the next couple of lines in that paragraph, too." The top section of his paper is turning light blue.

"There's another example farther down the page from Debater #2," Lydia says. "Do you see where they take Debater #1's point and twist it around to show companies wouldn't have to fire people if more people in our country have money to spend because that would help businesses? We should highlight that."

Matt nods. He highlights it.

I nod. I highlight it.

Matt points at another paragraph. "This part, where Debater #1 says Debater #2 is too soft and overdramatic and not paying attention to the numbers. That's one of those personal attacks Ms. Rochambeau doesn't want us to use, but they do seem to work. I don't know if we should highlight it."

"I bet Debater #2 is a girl and Debater #1 is a boy," Lydia says, rolling her eyes. "Girls are always being told they're too dramatic."

Matt laughs. "Whatever."

Lydia points her highlighter at him. "There's an example right there. Trying to dismiss what I say as not important."

"Aw, I was just kidding," Matt says. He glances at me like he's looking for support.

"That's another example," Lydia snaps. "Pretending not to be serious when you're called to account for your flaws, thereby trying to leave your opponent with only imaginary ground to stand on."

Matt looks over at me again.

Part of me wants to smile at him and send the message that I'm on his side, but the other part of me thinks that would be "another example" and Lydia would be snapping at me next.

And as much as I wanted to find out what it's like to be Matt, now I want to know what it's like to be Lydia even more.

"How's it going over here?" Ms. Rochambeau says, coming over to our table.

"It's good!" Matt says. He seems completely unfazed by the wagging highlighter of Lydia.

Ms. Rochambeau glances down at the highlighting on

Matt's sheet. "It looks like you're off to a fine start. Have you discussed the missed opportunities yet?"

Matt grins up at her. "We're just about to start."

Ms. Rochambeau nods and moves on to the table of eighth grade boys who are all standing up and yelling at each other.

"So what Debater #2 should have said after being called overdramatic," Lydia says, "is that the only person being over-dramatic is the person who thinks all businesses are going to collapse if workers get paid enough. And that if he thinks it's overdramatic to actually face the realities of what workers are—"

Matt cuts her off. "But if she says it like that, it'll just prove his point that she's overdramatic. She needs to . . ."

As Matt and Lydia go back and forth about what imaginary things these imaginary people could have said to each other, I sneak looks at both of them. Could I really be like them? I mean, an octopus can change colors ten times in a matter of seconds, so all sorts of ridiculous things are possible.

As I lean back, I overhear Kyla at the other table saying that if people always made a living wage, they'd be able to buy things like books for their kids to read, and how that'd be a good thing for the country.

I love my octopus book. Imagine if I had two.

I go to debate club on Wednesday, Thursday, and Friday, and nothing explodes. I don't ever actually say anything, but I pay attention and do the written parts. Ms. Rochambeau drives me home every day (her car smells like coffee), and I'm on time to pick up Bryce and Aurora. Plus, Ms. Rochambeau doesn't complain about it, and she doesn't push me about how quiet I am at debate club (and everywhere else) either. Maybe she feels bad about the "Suck it up" comment. I mean, she should. Instead, she talks about things she heard on the radio or saw on TV. Like stories about Peru where Connor had been, and documentaries about this kind of jellyfish that recycles its body as it ages, so unless it gets eaten by something else or smooshed or dries up, it never really dies.

I'm not about to get Frank to change the channel on his TV, but I kind of want to see for myself all the interesting bits she tells me about. Of course, I'm not about to tell Ms. Rochambeau that.

At debate club the following Monday when we're going to be brainstorming ideas that could be our "prepared topic" for the tournament, I take my seat and get out my notebook like I always do. I've started doing what Kyla does—writing lots of stuff down—and it seems like people do take you more seriously when you do that. And they don't ever ask to know what it says, so they can't tell you it's stupid.

"Remember," Ms. Rochambeau is saying, as she paces in front of the whiteboard with a marker in hand, "the topic has to be something where you can understand both sides of it because you don't know what position you're going to be assigned."

People start calling out possible topics to Ms. Rochambeau, and she writes each of them on the whiteboard almost as fast as they come. Mandatory recycling. Lowering the voting age to ten. Making voting required. Getting rid of speed limits. Drone strikes. Animal rights.

I'm writing them all down in my notebook, too, because why not?

Kyla raises her hand and adds, "Requiring the police to use body cameras," and "The effects of the private prison industry."

I don't know what the private prison industry is, but I write it down.

"Every school day includes a pie-eating contest!" calls out one of the eighth grade boys.

Ms. Rochambeau puts her hand on her hip and stops writing. "And what," she says, "do you propose would be the main arguments in favor?"

"Better attendance, of course," the boy says laughing. "And pie! Lots of pie!"

"And the argument against?"

"Umm . . . stomachaches?"

Ms. Rochambeau laughs. "We'll put it on the list. There's no wrong answer when you're brainstorming."

No wrong answer. Is that really true? Because part of me wants to raise my hand and get the topic about having enough money for new underwear and books added to the list. What was it called again? "Wage" something . . . I look back through my notebook to see if I can find it, but that was before I started writing things down.

I'm missing all of the new topics that are being added, but I can't raise my hand if I don't know what it's called . . . wage something. Something wage. Wait—it was living wage, wasn't it? I think it was.

I take a deep breath, and I raise my hand.

But before Ms. Rochambeau turns around to see it, something else happens.

"Attention! Attention!" an automated voice comes over the loudspeaker. "This is a lockdown. This is a lockdown. Follow lockdown protocols immediately. This is a lockdown. Follow lockdown protocols immediately."

I pull my hand back down to my side.

Ms. Rochambeau turns to us, her face pale, directs us to head to the far corner of the library near the biographies. Mr. Herd is up and moving, pulling down the shades for the windows that line the wall between the library and the main hallway. Is this a regular thing to do lockdown drills after school?

I follow Lydia and Matt and squeeze into a spot next to the *S* section of biographies. Lydia had the sense to bring her notebook with her, but she isn't drawing any cats. She's got her eyes closed tight. I'd be willing to guess after-school lockdown drills are *not* a thing.

Soon Mr. Herd joins us in the corner and crouches down, too. As he does, though, I see him and Ms. Rochambeau exchange a look. Definitely not a drill.

I try to focus on the row of books next to me. Shakespeare. Socrates. Sacagawea. Joseph Stalin. Elizabeth Cady Stanton. Henry Sampson. Molly Stark. William Tecumseh Sherman. Captain John Smith. Harriet Beecher Stowe.

All those people. All dead.

I glance over at Lydia's notebook. She's started drawing the cats again, but kind of in a frantic way. There are so many cats. Cats with stripes, cats with three eyes, a cat wearing a top hat.

Kyla is sitting one aisle over, but there are too many biographies in the way to tell if she's freaking out, too.

Even if everything is fine, what if we have to sit here so long that Ms. Rochambeau can't get me to the bus stop before Bryce and Aurora get off the bus? I close my eyes to try to block out the image of Aurora in the street with that car coming toward her and Bryce screaming from the side of the road, but it's no use.

And if everything isn't fine . . . I take a deep breath and try to keep my leg from going all jittery. I'm too close to everyone else to hide it if it does. If I'm going to die, I don't want to spend the last few minutes being embarrassed in the biography aisle.

I mean, we're probably not going to die, right? But still,

sometimes all it takes is being in the wrong place and you get way too close for comfort.

Suddenly, the night when I was four years old comes flooding back to me. My mom and I had been sleeping in our car for weeks, and I woke up to see a man's face at the window, trying to break in to steal all our stuff and maybe more. You might think that would mean lockdowns don't scare me as much. But they only scare me more.

Because I know how easy it can be for everything to suddenly become a nightmare.

I take a deep breath. But everything is going to be okay. I just have to get to Bryce and Aurora on time. I look around until I find the clock on the wall. 3:20. The seconds are ticking away far faster than they're supposed to.

In front of me, Matt is writing notes back and forth with Calvin Umbatoor on a single sheet of paper that's sitting on the floor between them.

This is super unfair.

> *I know. I have so many more good ideas*
> *for topics that I haven't gotten to say yet.*

Like what?

> *Whether we should colonize Mars.*

Because sulfur smells so great, right?

> *It would take lifetimes to get to a better*
> *planet.*

Not if we work on building a better rocket engine.

The writing keeps going, but I can't keep reading because my hand has started to shake and I have to bury it in my opposite elbow. So "super unfair" means not having time to discuss your Mars colonization ideas? Or maybe it's that the cherry on top of your ice cream sundae has dyed the whipped cream pink and you wanted it perfectly white?

I look back at the clock. 3:24.

I screamed when I saw that man's face at the window, and my mom woke up when I did. I never saw her move so fast. He shattered the window with his crowbar, but she beat him off with her keys until she could drive away. That little key chain against that big crowbar. But she was more motivated than he was. And she kept all sorts of sharp metal things on that keychain. I never wondered why again.

I can only see the back of Ms. Rochambeau's head. Can she see the clock from where she's sitting? Even if the voice over the intercom releases us like nothing happened, is she going to dawdle back over to the whiteboard and continue adding to the topic list?

I hear the pounding of someone sprinting down the hallway. Closer, closer, and then right past us on the way toward the office.

I catch Mr. Herd exchanging another glance with Ms. Rochambeau.

"May I have your attention please," Principal Fitzgerald's voice comes over the intercom. "There is no longer a threat to safety. I repeat: There is no longer a threat to safety. You may resume your earlier activities. Thank you for your patience."

As soon as the intercom clicks off, people are up and talking.

"What happened?"

"That wasn't a drill, was it?"

"Ms. Rochambeau?" an eighth grade girl asks. "Do you know what happened? Did they send you an email or something?"

Mr. Herd is already striding over to his computer. "I'm checking."

"Can't you go right down to the office and ask?" one of the eighth grade boys asks Ms. Rochambeau.

Ms. Rochambeau smooths her skirt and takes a deep breath. "The last thing they need right now is every teacher in the school showing up to demand an explanation of what just happened."

Mr. Herd is hunched over his computer. "There's no email yet. We'll just have to be okay with not knowing."

"Besides," Ms. Rochambeau says, looking at me, "it's almost 3:30 anyway. Most of you must have parents arriving to pick you up soon, and we all have places to get to. We'll meet back here again Wednesday afternoon and—"

No one hears what Ms. Rochambeau says next because Evan Hewitt bursts through the library doors. "Did you guys hear? Someone shot at someone in the parking lot!"

"Who?"

"Like with a gun?"

"Was it a student?"

"Did they miss or is someone like . . . *dead*?"

Kids immediately swarm around him, but I sink down into a chair. All I can see is that man's face pressed up against our car window. That split second it takes to go from safe to a full-on fight for survival.

"I heard that there was a kid involved, but I don't know who," Evan says. "I don't think anyone's hurt, because we could see some of the parking lot from where we were hiding in the cafeteria and no ambulance ever showed up. But yeah, it was a real gun. We heard the shots!"

Ms. Rochambeau has her hand over her mouth and her eyes on a chair that got knocked over when everyone stampeded over to Evan.

When she sees me looking at her, she quickly stands up straight, lowering her hand. "I'm glad no ambulance was needed," she says loud enough to quiet everyone else down, "but it will take us all a while to process this. Mr. Herd, will you help make sure that everyone's able to connect with their ride this afternoon?"

He nods and picks up his winter coat from where it's slung over his chair. "Of course."

"Thank you." Ms. Rochambeau turns to me. "We have to get going."

Silently, I collect my things and follow Ms. Rochambeau through the halls and out to the parking lot.

Everyone's okay. We're going to be on time to pick up Bryce and Aurora. It's all going to be okay.

Still I can't get the sound of our car window shattering that night out of my head.

I don't tell my mom about the lockdown when I bring along Bryce and Aurora to pick up Hector at the Pizza Pit. He's in the middle of yet another game of peekaboo with Connor and one of the customers. I guess my mom got some automated message on her cell phone later, though, because she calls Frank's TracFone from the restaurant and asks him to put me on the line.

"Why didn't you tell me what happened?" she snaps.

Frank is glowering at me like he's going to grab the phone back any second.

"I didn't want to bother you." I turn around so I don't have to stare at Frank while I talk. Aurora and Bryce are screaming about lightsabers in the bedroom, and Hector is flinging Cheerios out of his tray.

"You could have gotten killed!" my mom yells.

Where could she be standing in the restaurant and be able to yell like that? Is she in the walk-in fridge?

"I wasn't even in the parking lot," I say. "I didn't even see the person who had the gun. What'd they say on the message? Do they know who it was?" I peer around Lenny's nice curtains to look out the window.

"They didn't say anything on that stupid message except that there had been shots fired in the parking lot and that no one was hurt and that the police were conducting a full investigation. Because that takes care of everything, doesn't it?"

The icicles hanging off the neighbor's roof have gotten even bigger in the last few days. She doesn't need a motion-sensor light for safety. She's got daggers ready to cut down anyone who dares to come too close.

My mom is still talking, but I hear a sharp "Time's up" from behind me. I turn to see Frank, still glowering at me and now tapping his wrist.

"Mom, I gotta go." I hang up and hand the phone back to him. "Thanks for letting me use it."

"So, what's all this about a gun?" He says it so slowly that it's like he's narrating the documentary about the Civil War that Ms. Rochambeau had us watch.

"There were gunshots heard in the school parking lot after school today."

"You wait," Frank says, just as slow. I can almost hear the documentary's mournful violin background music start up. He leans forward. "They're all going to get their panties in a bunch and start blaming guns like they're the devil incarnate, just like they did at those public hearings a year ago. They'll be knocking down our door trying to take ours away before you know it."

He sinks back down into his recliner and keeps glaring at me like I'm the one showing up to steal his old .22 rifle. "They don't know anything about guns, but they sure like to act like they do. Like they know everything about everything." Frank pulls out a new strand of cinnamon floss and yanks it free. "They think we're too stupid to take care of ourselves." He settles back in to floss his teeth and watch another history documentary. "Just try to come and get it," he mumbles to no one in particular. "Just try."

That doesn't make me feel any better.

CHAPTER 16

On my way to the bus stop the next morning, I see Silas com-
ing out of his trailer.

"Hey," I call as he comes down the steps.

He doesn't answer. He just climbs over the mountain of
snow left by the snowplow. When he hits the road, he keeps
his head down, his camo trucker hat pulled way farther down
than normal.

"Silas?" I ask. "Are you okay?"

No answer. It's like he switched into mute mode early.

He walks right past me like he doesn't even see me.

Fuchsia doesn't have a mute mode. She appears next to
my locker before I've even gotten to the second number of my
locker combination.

"Ugh," she says, leaning against a locker. She sighs. She rolls her eyes.

I take off my jacket. "Did you hear what happened after school yesterday?"

She sighs again.

I glare into my locker, but the words I'm supposed to say slip out anyway. "What's wrong?"

"I had the worst asthma attack last night."

And I was a couple hundred feet away from a shooter, but does she care about that? I start shoving my jacket into my locker.

She sighs a third time. I keep trying to squish my jacket in.

"Are you okay?" I ask.

"I almost had to go to the emergency room. It was horrible." Fuchsia stares up at the ceiling. "I can still feel it in my chest. It's like it's ready to tighten up any second to stop me from breathing."

"Why are you even at school then?"

She glares at me. "I'm on my way to the nurse to make sure she has my inhaler like I'm supposed to, and what's wrong with you?"

I shake my head. "Maybe the inhaler will help," I mutter. *Because you need loads of help.*

Fuchsia snorts as she pushes herself back up. "Yeah right." She starts heading for the nurse. "Thanks for the support," she calls.

When I was five we rented a room in a house with chickens in the backyard, and entering homeroom is like walking through that flock of chickens as they pecked all over the place to get every possible bit of corn. Except instead of corn it's any bit of detail or rumor or possibility of what might have happened yesterday afternoon in the parking lot.

Mr. Bontaff is nowhere to be seen.

Brendan Farley is pacing around in the front of the room. "It was three separate shots, and one of those bullets went right by my head! I swear I heard it zing past me."

"Where were they coming from?" Matt is leaning up against the whiteboard. "They didn't say on the news report last night. Did you see the gun?"

Brendan doesn't stop pacing. "No, but there were plenty of places someone could have been hiding in the parking lot."

"Who else was there?" Calvin Umbatoor asks.

"There was a car whose window got shot out, but I don't know whose it was. It drove away as soon as it happened, and I don't blame them." Brendan stops his pacing. "You know who I think was the shooter?"

Calvin looks up. "Who?"

I try to make my way to a seat in the back.

Brendan's voice is loud enough for the whole homeroom to hear. "Silas Fletcher."

I freeze.

"I mean, he never talks, right?" Brendan continues. "He could totally be one of those mass murderers that you hear about when they interview the neighbors and they're like 'Oh, he was always quiet. Never thought he'd do something like this.'"

So being quiet is suddenly the same as being a school shooter?

"*And*," Brendan says, "it was just a couple weeks ago that he got in trouble for having a gun in the parking lot. And right in that very same corner of the parking lot. I mean, it's obvious."

Because he was going hunting! For bobcats! Where you're supposed to be quiet!

Calvin is on his feet. "You know, he's always been weird. I don't trust him at all."

Matt is leaning against the whiteboard, silent. At least he's not jumping on board like Calvin is.

But then he slowly nods his head. "I can totally see him turning on someone out of the blue like that."

What is wrong with these people? Doesn't Brendan remember that it was right after he teased Silas for crying in fifth grade that Silas stopped talking? I was there, and it was obvious. Doesn't he get it that if someone lines up people to place bets on your "time-to-cry" you might decide to zip your real self up and not come out again?

And just because he yanked that zipper up doesn't mean that three years later he's going to turn around and start shooting at people. Even if they're the people who bullied him before.

Right?

I mean, he was all weird and mute this morning, but that doesn't mean anything.

Right?

"Alright, ladies and gentlemen. Have a seat." I turn to see Mr. Bontaff in the doorway. "We have something we need to talk about."

I hustle to a seat in the back and keep my head down. If Mr. Bontaff is about to say that Silas Fletcher was the shooter yesterday I don't want to see him do it. Maybe I can block my ears and pretend nothing happened at all.

"You may or may not be aware of the events that occurred in the parking lot yesterday afternoon . . ." begins Mr. Bontaff, who then proceeds to tell us even less than we already know. To make things even worse, he encourages people who may know something about the event to come forward and speak with the administration—and says that your identity will be protected if you do.

Brendan already has his hand up.

He might as well be holding a torch in one hand and a pitchfork in the other.

The whole rest of the school day is like that. By lunchtime, the entire seventh grade class is obsessed with the idea that Silas was the shooter. Even the girls at the lunch table are talking about it. And they're nothing like Brendan Farley and Matt Hubbard, who always act like they know what's going on. They tuck their heads and don't get involved. Like when those public hearings about guns happened last year, their families were nowhere to be seen—even though they were the ones that probably should have been right in the middle of it, since their families hunt and they aren't terrified of guns like some of the other kids.

By the first period after lunch nobody even has to be convinced anymore. They've all moved on to talking about when he's going to get called down to the principal's office or making plans for how they'll take him down if he tries to go all *Call of Duty* on them. I heard that a couple of girls started crying and refused to be in the same room as Silas during English class.

The only part of the day that's about something different is when Ms. Rochambeau pulls me aside after social studies. "I want to make sure you're still planning to go to tomorrow's debate club," she says.

I've been going for the past week, haven't I?

She keeps on talking. "And this time I want you to come ready to speak up. I think your viewpoint is going to be particularly valuable."

I swallow. Speaking up is a different story.

The next day, most of the debate club kids are already in their seats when I ease myself into the chair next to Lydia, who's back to drawing cats. Matt is leaning over another table, but when Ms. Rochambeau calls everyone to attention, he quickly takes his seat.

"As you know, we ran out of time on Monday, and we weren't able to vote on a topic," she says. "I've decided to choose it myself, but I think you'll agree we don't have any other option." She turns to write on the board.

Resolved: The right to own a gun is part of what it means to be an American.

No one says anything at first. Not even the eighth grade boy who had fifty different ideas for topics two days ago.

Lydia has stopped drawing cats. "I can sure argue against that, but we'll have to argue for that, too?"

Ms. Rochambeau crosses her arms. "That is the point."

No one says much as Ms. Rochambeau points to a list of websites up on the board. "These will have relevant statistics and ideas for talking points to help you get started. You'll be working in your table groups to prepare, and then tomorrow I'll be selecting one person from each table to take part in our mock debate."

There are three laptops at our table already, and Matt pulls one of them over toward him. "I'll check out the Center for

Disease Control first. You guys should start with the others, so we can share notes."

I'm still frozen in place from Ms. Rochambeau's words. She wouldn't choose me to be in the mock debate, would she? I sneak a peek at her, leaning over one of the eighth grade boy's notebooks and pointing out "a few gaps in the logic here."

She totally would.

I look around, starting to panic. Lydia has pushed a laptop over to me, and I open it, but I can feel my octopus skin turning all agitated and red. I quickly type in the web address for the Bureau of Alcohol, Tobacco, and Firearms that's listed on the board.

"Oh my gosh," Matt says, staring at his screen. "Look at how many more people die because of guns in the US compared to the rest of the world. It's like we're living in a war zone."

I try to stay in control of my breathing. I peer over at his screen. There's a bunch of bar graphs, but I don't want to take the time to figure out what each bar means because I just want to say, "Oh yeah, you're so right."

And I do.

Matt nods and starts writing things in his notebook.

I've found my way to the Firearms Frequently Asked Questions part of the site, but it's ten pages long, is super duper detailed about stuff I've never heard of, and doesn't have any cool graphs like Matt found.

But Matt is copying stuff down into his notebook like a madman, so I pick an FAQ at random and just start copying its answer down. At least I'll have something. I do my best to ignore the fact that my leg is starting to go all jittery.

I'm halfway through writing out the question: *Is there a way for a prohibited person to restore his or her right to receive or possess firearms or ammunition?*—when Lydia interrupts.

"I mean, this whole thing is ridiculous," she explodes. "Look at the pictures of these kids who've been killed. If we'd been in that parking lot at the wrong time, we could have been pictures on this website. It could have been our parents talking about how we were always being kind to other people and worked hard and all that. I can't believe we're going to have to argue both sides of this. No one should have guns."

Is she serious? What about the nice girls at the lunch table whose families hunt?

"Yeah," Matt says, copying one of the bar graphs into his notebook, "it's like arguing both sides of a resolution about how puppies should or shouldn't be put to death. One side is right, and the other is evil."

I sit on my hand because it's started to shake, too.

Lydia rubs her forehead. "I just don't get why when it comes to guns our country is like, 'Oh yeah, take that thing that's used to kill people and do whatever you want with it.'"

"Well, except for the laws against murder and stuff," I blurt out.

Lydia doesn't take her eyes off her laptop screen. "Come on. If people didn't have guns in the first place, we'd be way better off."

I loved going hunting. Would Silas be better off if his family didn't have guns? He wouldn't be in this mess, but then he wouldn't get to go bobcat hunting with his dad either. And if someone is going to be miserable every school day, they shouldn't have to lose the one thing that makes them happy.

I eye Lydia. She probably wants me to keep my mouth shut, but isn't the whole point of debate club to argue? Ms. Rochambeau even told me to speak up, right?

I touch my shoulder to be close to my octopus tattoo and imagine my tentacles reaching out to cover Lydia's notebook and suck up some of its confidence. I take a deep breath. "Except most people with guns aren't using them to kill people," I say. "Don't you think it's a little drastic to—"

Lydia snaps at me. "Are you for real? Drastic? Don't you think it's a little drastic for people to *die* because of guns?"

I feel my mouth drop open, but before I have time to think of anything to say in response—anything about responsible gun owners or about how the deer population would be through the roof if it wasn't for hunters, Lydia's eyes fall on my camo jacket that's lying next to my chair. Her lips purse and her face goes stiff. "Oh, I get it," she says slowly. "You're one of them."

One of them? One of who?

Then, suddenly, those words "Your viewpoint is going to be particularly valuable" take on a whole new meaning. I'm supposed to be the evil one.

And maybe I am. Maybe Silas is, too. Maybe he really did shoot at someone in the parking lot. And I'm the one who told him he better keep hunting.

I look at Matt, but he isn't paying any attention. Instead, he's busy copying something down from the computer. "Seven kids killed by guns in this country every single day," he's muttering. "I might be able to find some bizarre way to argue for this resolution if I have to but . . ." He stares at what he's just written. "Anyone who really agrees with it either is as dumb as a rock or a straight-up monster."

Right.

I kick my camo jacket farther under my chair.

So, dumb rock or monster. It's good to know I have options.

CHAPTER 17

I'm too angry to talk to Ms. Rochambeau during the ride to Bryce and Aurora's bus stop. Of all issues to pick, did it really have to be this one? Where's our innocent discussion about the effectiveness of speed limits? Where are the pie-eating contests?

Since my mom doesn't work today because of Hector's nine-month checkup at the doctor, Bryce and Aurora are getting off at the bus stop near the entrance to the trailer park, and I have Ms. Rochambeau stop there.

"Right here?" she says, looking around. "I see . . . " She trails off, and before she can hide it I see the pity on her face. And those are the trailers with nice potted plants and decorative walkway lights that she's looking at. I get out of the car as quickly as I can, and mumble "thanks" as I go—but she doesn't drive away.

She's still sitting there parked on the side of the road when Bryce and Aurora's bus pulls up. She's not looking down at her phone either, she's watching. Maybe it's not in a judgy way, but why wouldn't it be?

I can feel her eyes on us as Bryce and then Aurora start spilling down the bus steps. Suddenly all I can see is their gray-tinged clothes that smell like Frank's cigarette smoke and their ratty hair that never got combed in the morning. If the other kids at their school haven't yet decided that they must either be dumb as a rock or a monster, then it's just a matter of time.

As soon as Bryce hits the ground, he starts kicking at ice chunks. Kick. An ice chunk goes spinning into the bus's wheel. Kick. An ice chunk sails into the street. Kick.

"Come on, Bryce. You need to be on the sidewalk."

I help Aurora jump down the last step off the bus, and she suctions herself onto me.

Future octopus.

Bryce is still on the edge of the road, kicking whatever he can kick.

"Bryce! Come on!"

Kick. Kick. Kick.

Ms. Rochambeau is still watching us.

"Let's go home and get you a snack."

"NO!"

"You've got to get out of the street."

"NO!"

"Okay. I get it. You had a bad day, but—"

"Stupid!"

I pry Aurora off my leg, but since we don't have Hector with us that means she instantly wants to be picked up. I hoist her up onto my hip and start walking away from the trailer park. "We're going to the Cumberland Farms," I call back to Bryce. "You better come, too, if you want some Easy Cheese."

I walk on without looking back. At least at first. When I peek half a minute later, Bryce is shuffling along behind us.

Only then does Ms. Rochambeau finally drive away. Guess she's seen enough. Except that when she passes us, she does something I'm not expecting.

She gives me a thumbs-up.

A thumbs-up.

Which actually feels even better than Easy Cheese tastes.

At Cumberland Farms, I slip the Easy Cheese can into my coat pocket when Aurora and Bryce are distracted by the frosted donuts near the hot dogs. Then I pick up a roll of toilet paper, because we're almost out, and I pay the cashier for that. I don't want Bryce and Aurora to think you're not supposed to pay for things—unless you really can't.

On the walk home from the Cumberland Farms, Bryce is more like his normal self. He insists on holding Aurora's hand and helping her around a patch of black ice. He doesn't do it in a bossy way either. The anticipation of Easy Cheese creates its own miracles.

When we get home to the trailer, Lenny is closed off in his bedroom instead of at work, and Frank says something about him being sick. So, I herd my screaming monkeys into our bedroom for our Easy Cheese picnic to keep them from waking him up if he's sleeping, and we have a happy, whispering time making an Easy Cheese *A* for Aurora and an Easy Cheese *B* for Bryce and an Easy Cheese *H* for Hector and an Easy Cheese *Z* for Zoey. And an Easy Cheese *E* for Easy Cheese. But it doesn't last. Bryce wants to make an *S* for Stupid, and then things get worse from there. They yell at each other. They yell at me. They yell at the bedroom lamp because they don't like its shape.

Because they couldn't be upset about something rational like Frank's constant smoking or the fact that the three of us have to share a room together.

No, it's the shape of the bedroom lamp that's the real evil in the world.

We get to have hamburgers for dinner, though, because at least there's plenty of ground beef.

When they're finally asleep—thankfully Frank's angry news program works even better than a story tonight—I carry them one at a time from the couch into their bed. I stare at their faces next to each other on the pillow, so quiet and peaceful, before any of Bryce's nightmares have had time to grab hold. And then I find myself digging down through a pile of stuff on the floor until my hand closes around their comb. I perch on the side of their bed, and even though it risks waking them up, I can't help myself: I start combing their hair. I comb all the hair I can reach, and then I shimmy some more of Aurora's out from where it was smushed against the pillow and comb that, too.

Even though their hair will be back to being all ratty in the morning.

Even though it won't be enough to stop other kids from saying things about them.

Still, I comb.

When I finally head back out to the main room, Frank has fallen asleep. I turn off the TV, and as soon as the sound cuts out, I hear something else: voices through the wall. It's my mom and Lenny arguing again. They've been in there together since dinner, so she could supposedly take care of Lenny.

The voices don't sound like anyone is sick, though.

A moment later I'm climbing back up onto the washing

machine, and putting my unblinking octopus eye against the hole.

Lenny is pacing again. "You're the one who's got to answer for all of this. What was I supposed to think when I got into the car to drive to work and it's almost on empty? How far can you drive in the two hours between my jobs?"

My mom is already crying. "I had to go to the pharmacy. And then to the grocery store. And then there were problems with our EBT card, and I had to hurry back home to get some paperwork for them, so it'd go through. And I didn't think to look at the gas tank because I just thought it was real important to buy . . ."

Ground beef.

"Yeah, you didn't think, did you? You never do! And now we're out two hundred and seventy dollars a week because of you."

Wait. Two hundred and seventy dollars a week? Did Lenny lose his job?

My mom is shaking her head. "I don't see how the gas has anything to do with—"

"I had just had to drive to work on fumes! My girlfriend couldn't even do a simple thing like not use up all the gas in the car—and I'm somehow supposed to 'stay calm' after that when I've got a patient yelling at me that the trash smells? Who wouldn't snap back?"

My mom swallows. "But you didn't have to get so upset. You know you can't yell at a patient like that because then—"

"What? Is Little Miss Clueless going to tell me what I should have said instead?"

I cringe as I watch my mom, Little Miss Clueless, shake her head as she turns to face the wall. Her mouth is stretched out like it's all she can do to hold back a mountain of sobbing.

Little Miss Clueless.

And then I realize: Lenny is saying that on purpose. He knows what he's doing.

He's discrediting his opponent.

"Cry me a river, why don't you?" he sneers. "You just want to manipulate this whole thing so it looks like it wasn't your fault. Well, sorry! A million tears don't change anything. They don't change reality."

Whose reality?

"What are we going to do?" my mom murmurs to the wall. "I was just about to start saving up for the down payment on a new washing machine, but . . ."

"You should have thought of that when you used up all the gas in the car."

"I just thought . . . I just thought . . ."

"What? What did you think?"

"I just thought you said I should get more ground beef!"

"How dare you try to turn this around on me," snaps

Lenny. "When did I say that you should use up all the gas in the car just to buy stupid ground beef?"

My mom turns away from the wall to look at Lenny. Like maybe he's kidding. Like maybe she's not going crazy. She opens her mouth, but then she closes it again.

Because what's the point? She's Little Miss Clueless.

I press my hand against my octopus tattoo. No. She isn't.

CHAPTER 18

The next morning it's not snowing exactly, more like icing, and the wind is squeezing between the tightly packed trailers. Up ahead I see Silas coming down his trailer steps. He has his hat pulled down low, mute-mode style, and slowly plods forward. A death march to the bus stop.

If he was the shooter, the school or the police haven't been able to prove it yet, because he wouldn't be walking to the bus stop at all. He'd already be on his way to juvie. But that hardly matters because the judgment has already been handed down. Most of the seventh grade has already decided that he's so different from them that they can imagine him trying to kill someone.

And why not lump in the rest of us dumb-as-rocks monsters.

Clearly we're not fit to breathe the same air as them. And what if they're right?

After school Matt and Lydia are already in their seats when I get to the library. This time in the empty space in the middle of the library there are two lone music stands facing each other.

"So, today," Ms. Rochambeau starts off, "you'll have just ten more minutes in your table groups to prepare your arguments, and then we'll get to our first mock debate." She walks over to the music stands. "These are our podiums, but no pressure. You don't have to sing." She's made a joke, but she's the kind of person who doesn't even crack a smile, so it's not that obvious.

Kyla raises her hand. "Ms. Rochambeau, are we just supposed to talk about regular people killing people, or are we going to talk about the times when cops kill people, like black people specifically?"

I look at her. Really? Cops don't kill people, do they? Life is hard enough as it is.

Ms. Rochambeau raises her eyebrows, but it isn't the Raised Eyebrow of Disappointment—it's like a Raised Eyebrow of Very Impressed.

"That is a very good question, and you can most definitely bring it up in your debate." She pauses and looks at the rest of us. "Maybe we should even have our next debate topic focused entirely on that. There are plenty of examples to discuss."

So wait, that's true? Cops have really killed black people? How can that be a thing—a thing that has 'plenty of examples'?

"Okay," Ms. Rochambeau is saying, "I'm going to tell you who our first debate participants will be, but I'm not going to tell you which side they'll be presenting yet. Lucas . . ." Over at the eighth grade boys' table one of them leaps out of his chair with a "YES!" and does a little dance like he just scored a touch-down. "And . . ." Ms. Rochambeau eyes our table. "Zoey."

Lydia glares up at Ms. Rochambeau. "Seriously?" she mutters under her breath.

Matt crosses his arms. "Oh, that is so not fair." He turns to me. "I mean, no offense."

I don't say anything. Mostly I'm trying to melt into the floor.

"Well, at least it'll be easy for you if you get assigned the pro-gun side, right?" Lydia says with a smirk. "Here, I copied down a bunch of the ridiculous talking points from the NRA website last night at home. You can copy them into your note-book unless you already have them memorized." She shoves her notebook toward me. "And the page before is the reasons why guns are evil. I'd copy those points down, too, just so you're ready—and so you can try to fit them into your brain," she adds under her breath.

I force myself to take her notebook and skim the bullet points she's written out: *the only thing that stops a bad guy with a gun is a good guy with a gun . . . protection against a tyrannical government . . .* All lines that I can hear Frank saying word for word.

I try to keep reading, but I can't. It's not just having to stand up and talk in front of people. It's having to say words that people are already sure you believe—when *you're* not sure at all.

Because since when does "life, liberty, and the pursuit of happiness" mean "prepare yourself for a shoot-out"?

I flip to the page before it, to what Matt and Lydia both think . . . *evil killing machines . . .*

I don't think that either. Is a fishing rod evil because it catches someone's dinner? No. It's a tool. Just the way a gun is. Just the way a chain saw is. Just don't give it to the wrong person.

I keep reading what it says . . . *why would any moral person need a gun when it's clear that too many people are dying?*

I think about the faces of the kids on that website Lydia pulled up and close my eyes. I don't want anyone to die. Maybe I should just believe what they say about guns. Believe what they say about Silas. Believe what they say about me.

I wanted to be like Matt and Lydia. With their notes and their laptops and their smug little faces. All so confident that they're right.

All looking down on me.

Little Miss Clueless.

No.

The word comes from deep inside me.

I touch my octopus tattoo. I refuse to get put in a box. I refuse to stay trapped.

I am an octopus.

I stand up from my chair, and Lydia looks up at me with a start. But when I grab my jacket and backpack, she sure doesn't stop me. And I walk out.

"Zoey?" Ms. Rochambeau calls after me.

But I don't stop, and when I get out the door and around the corner, I run.

I run down the hall and out the double doors by the office. I don't stop running until I've reached the far side of the parking lot.

I drop my jacket and backpack down onto the snow. Where am I even going?

I glance back at the door. No one has followed me out.

Was that standing up for myself or just running away?

The wind whips around me. This is where I need Ms. Rochambeau to drive me across town.

But the only thing I know for sure is that there's no way I'm crawling back, groveling, to ask for a measly ride.

I pick up my coat, pull it on, and then I swing my backpack over my shoulder and shove my hands in my pockets.

I'll walk.

I get home with twenty minutes to spare, but my feet feel like toeless blocks of ice. All I want to do is curl up on the couch and watch that angry guy news program with Frank. Except he isn't here. And then I remember it's the monthly bingo tournament at the senior center.

I look around at the perfectly aligned end tables and the alphabetized collection of DVDs, but instead of feeling good, all I feel is Lenny. And those words: Little Miss Clueless.

Like a giant foot on top of us.

Who cares if his feet are clean and his toenails are clipped just so?

Who cares if his movies are alphabetized?

Who cares if his undershirt drawer is perfectly organized?

I push into Lenny's bedroom without even taking my coat off and pull open that stupid undershirt drawer. And before I even know what I'm doing all of my tentacles are grabbing at the shirts, pulling them out of their perfectly folded squares, yanking them out and flinging them around the room. The perfectly organized room where he tells my mom *and convinces her* that she's worthless.

I fall back onto the bed amid the scattered undershirts and squeeze my eyes shut.

My mom was right, of course. Nothing's going to change.

Why can't I just accept that?

I turn and glare at one of the undershirts next to me. Like I have to pick all of these undershirts back up because otherwise he's just going to take it out on my mom.

I can't glare at them hard enough. I want to squirt my black octopus ink all over them.

I finally push myself up to sitting. I pull the closest undershirt over and smooth it out like he does to get ready to fold it. It isn't until I see spots of wetness dotting the undershirt that I realize I'm crying.

I fold every single one of those stupid undershirts. I fold them into those stupid squares he cares so much about.

And I hate myself for doing it.

I turn back to the open drawer. That's when I see it. In the far back corner, tucked under the only remaining undershirt.

A piece of paper.

As soon as I've got it partway open, I know exactly what it is.

The form for the power company. The one my mom spent a whole day filling out. The one that Lenny swore he turned in.

By why would he turn it in? When not turning it in would be such a good reminder for my mom of her incompetence.

My hand is shaking as I fold it up and stuff it in my back pocket, but this time it's a good kind of shaking.

Because when I watch my mom argue with Lenny it's like watching her try to grab hold of a blob of grape jelly. No matter where she tries to grab it, it splurches out around her fingers.

But this. This is the evidence that supports her position. The blob of jelly has become a solid Jell-O popsicle. Not only can you can pick it up, but you can wave it around.

And that's what I intend to do.

CHAPTER 19

When I get to the Pizza Pit, Connor is sitting in a booth with one of the regulars and has Hector on his lap. My mom comes out of the kitchen when she hears the bell on the door jingle. She reaches for the menus like she's ready to seat me before she realizes it's me. "Oh!" She glances back at Connor. "I thought today was one of your get-home-late days."

"It was," I say. "But I'm here now. I need to talk to you."

"What? What's wrong?"

"I was thinking we could go somewhere private," I say, looking around. "Maybe the bathroom?"

My mom glares at me because clearly I've done something horrible to warrant having to hide in the bathroom to talk about it. She drops the menus back onto the hostess stand. "You've only got three minutes."

"I know."

As soon as we're both in the bathroom, she pulls the door shut behind us. Ricky has never been much of a decorator, but there is one black-and-white photo of a funny-looking car on the wall. Maybe it's supposed to be an Italian car, but I'm not sure.

"Okay . . . so . . . " I stammer. Who thought this was a good idea? Maybe I can make up something different to tell her.

I finger the folded-up form in my pocket. No. This is about not letting people mess with you. Maybe it's going to be awkward, but Ms. Rochambeau would probably just tell me to suck it up.

"You know that hole in the wall over the washing machine," I start. "You can see into your bedroom through it."

"Are you serious, Zoey? This is what you need to tell me?" My mom starts fixing her makeup in the mirror.

"And I saw the way Lenny blamed you that night we lost power and . . . "

"You've been spying on us?"

I take a deep breath, "And how he keeps doing it. Blaming you for every—"

"That is none of your business," my mom snaps. "And, of all people, you know how lucky we are to get to live with him. It's not like he hits me. We are *lucky*."

"But the way he treats you, Mom!"

She bares her teeth to the mirror and wipes a smudge of

pink lipstick off one of them. "He just gets frustrated some-times. He's allowed to get frustrated like anyone."

"He doesn't have to take it out on you!"

She shrugs. "Well, when it's my fault, it makes sense."

"Except when it isn't." I pull out the form from my pocket and hand it to her.

She unfolds it and stares at it. "How do you have this?"

"He had it, Mom. He had it all along. He never turned it in like he said he did."

My mom looks up at me, and her eyes are like firebolts. I'm ready for this. I'm ready for her to be furious with him. I'm ready to hug her and tell her that I love her and that I'm so sorry she's having to live with this.

"How . . . dare . . . you," she says.

Me? How dare *me*?

"How dare you give this to me? What are you trying to do? Stir up trouble?"

"What?" I sputter. "No! I'm not trying to make trouble. I just wanted you to know the truth!"

Her eyes widen, and I hardly see her hand slicing through the air before the slap lands on my cheek, hard, angry, and stinging.

"You want the truth?" she snarls as she rips up the form and hurls it into the trash. "Here's the truth: if I catch you spying on us ever again you'll regret it for the rest of your life!" She pulls open the bathroom door and storms out.

I sink down onto the toilet.

Alone.

Thursdays are my mom's short shift because it's trivia night at the Pizza Pit and Ricky likes to work the floor himself those nights. My mom doesn't look at me when she gets home, though. Just bustles right into the kitchen, pulls out a box of spaghetti, and puts water on to boil.

"You home, Mommy!" Aurora squeals and runs over to hug her. "Are we gonna have 'paghetti?"

My mom leans down to hug Aurora. "We sure are." She nods to Bryce who's skulking up behind them like he wants to hug her, but he doesn't think he should.

"How was your day at school, Bryce?" she asks.

He shrugs. "Okay."

Once the pot is on the stove, she pulls out the stuff to make Hector's formula. She still doesn't look at me.

I pick up Hector out of his seat and plop down on the couch with him like all I want to do is hold him and watch TV with Frank. No big deal, right? What did I expect her to do when I confronted her? Just instantly go back to the determined, fearless mama bear she was when I was eight?

Maybe she was never that different from how she is now. Maybe I was just too young to know better.

Frank is watching *The Lost Secrets of the War of 1812*, but even though the volume is up, I can still hear Aurora helping my mom in the kitchen like they're a totally normal family.

"Are we going to have 'paghetti sauce, too?"

"Can I 'tir it?"

"Oh yum! Are those meatballs?"

"What's that out the window?"

I peek over and see Aurora hopping up and down at my mom's feet. Bryce is slouching by the refrigerator, playing with the can opener.

My mom peers out the window over the sink. "Oh, you're right, Aurora. A bird just flew by. One of those little chickadee birds."

"Chick-a-DEEDEEDEEDEEEDEE!" Aurora screams, flapping her arms like wings.

"My little chickadee," my mom laughs, patting Aurora on the head.

Of all times for Frank to turn up the TV to drown them out, couldn't this be it?

I hear the door and then Lenny's voice: "It sure is good to smell dinner cooking when you get home!" Lenny walks in, his perfectly shaved cheeks practically shining.

"How was your day?" my mom asks him. She has a smile

on like Lenny had a normal day, and not a first day of being partially unemployed.

Lenny stretches. "Pretty good. Filled out some applications. No bites yet, but I'll keep trying."

"I just know there's going to be someone who can't wait to hire you." My mom leans up against the sink and peers out the window. "Oh, the chickadee is back! It's got its feathers all puffed out like a big puffy coat. It's so cute!"

"No one cares about some bird, so settle down," Lenny says. "And the pasta is boiling over."

"Oh!" my mom exclaims, reaching to switch off the burner and uncover the pot as the water comes streaming down the sides.

Lenny shakes his head and tosses her the roll of paper towels. "Make sure you get all that junk out from under the burner. I'm going to go take a shower."

My mom might be scurrying around in a paper-towel tizzy, trying to clean up all the boiling hot water, but Bryce is like a statue as he watches Lenny head into the bathroom. Even after Lenny closes the door behind him, Bryce still doesn't move.

I put Hector on my hip and quietly approach Bryce. I put my free arm around him. "Come on," I whisper. "Let's see if we can get Hector to giggle."

But Bryce just shakes his head, slips out from under my arm, and goes back to fiddling with the can opener.

"Zoey, look!" Aurora calls. "I'm 'tirring the 'paghetti!"

I take a deep breath. Bryce is hunched over the can opener, spinning it and spinning it and spinning it.

"Zoey," Aurora calls again. "You have to come see!"

I nod. "I'm coming."

Twenty minutes later, the stove has been perfectly cleaned and my mom is pouring milk into cups for the kids. I've put Hector back in his seat and am separating the meatballs from the sauce on Aurora's plate because she doesn't like them touching—when Lenny reemerges from the bathroom. He's stroking his cheek like he might have just shaved for the second time today. Like a perfectly shaven cheek is how you get to some perfect heaven. And like he's on his way there, happily dragging my mom behind him by her hair.

She chose him over me. Him and his perfectly shaved cheek.

I want to tackle him. I want to knock him down.

I straighten up and face him. "I joined the debate club at school."

The words come out of my mouth before I can stop them. And, of course, I don't even know if I'm in the club anymore since I just walked out, but if there was a debate club where you got to debate Lenny, I'd be all over it.

He smirks and shakes his head. "Right."

"I did," I say.

He's about to pull the fridge open, but he stops and looks

at me like I'm some little girl hiding an ice cream cone behind my back. "You really expect me to believe that?"

I'm not going to let him throw me off. "The teacher in charge of the club is even giving me a ride home so I can pick up Bryce and Aurora on time."

"Yeah, I know that's what you told your mom, but I'm not as gullible as she is." He raises his eyebrows at me like we're sharing some special secret. "I know you and your little friends just want more time to get into stuff you shouldn't be getting into."

"How can you—"

"You can argue all you want, little lady," he says, opening the fridge and grabbing his can of soda, "but it's only going to prove you're trying to make trouble."

I open my mouth but no words come out. I catch my mom watching. Her face looks gray.

Aurora tugs at my shirt. "Is my 'paghetti ready? I'm hungry."

I nod and slide her plate off the counter, so she can bring it with her to the couch.

It's twenty minutes later when we're watching the local news that I realize what should have come out of my mouth. "You know that you're just trying to discredit your opponent. I learned that at debate club."

Except that it didn't.

There are so many reasons why I don't belong in debate club.

Later that evening, after getting Hector to sleep, my mom and Lenny have gone out to the pool hall to see some of Lenny's friends. Bryce and Aurora are zoned out in front of the TV.

"Alright, come on guys," I call. "Time to get ready for bed."

Neither of them say anything in response or even move. Frank's currently watching one of those political analysis shows, so there's no way they're really paying attention to it. I put down the dish I've been washing and walk behind the couch to lean over right between their heads. "Bryce and Aurora, it's time to get up and get ready for bed."

Bryce glances at me and then looks back at the TV. "No one cares about listening to you, so settle down."

I freeze. Maybe it's Bryce sitting there, but it's Lenny's words coming out of his mouth.

I'm sitting next to him in an instant. "Don't you dare start saying what Lenny says," I whisper.

He glares at me. "What's wrong with it?"

"Because Lenny's not being nice when he says things like that," I hiss. "Don't be like that."

Bryce crosses his arms and his voice comes out loud enough to shake the whole trailer. "I will be if I want to be!"

"'Top yelling," Aurora says. "You too loud."

"I'm not yelling," he screams.

Aurora stamps her foot. "Yes you are!"

"BOTH OF YOU NEED TO SHUT UP!" erupts Mount Frank from his recliner.

Bryce and Aurora immediately burst into tears and make a break for the bedroom, wailing.

When I come through the door after them, Bryce has turned to Aurora. "You don't know anything," he snaps at her through his tears. "You know less than nothing. You're just a stupid bug that keeps annoying everyone around you. And no one cares about you."

"Bryce Albro!" I cry. "What's the matter with you?" They fight all the time, but it's about who gets to play with what toy or who accidentally pushed whom. It's never flat-out mean.

Aurora's tears keep flowing, but it's a silent kind of crying now. She's almost trembling as she stares at her older brother.

I kneel down to be face-to-face with her. "It's not true what he said." I wipe a tear from her cheek. "You need to know it's not true."

She lets me pick her up and burrows her head into my shoulder. "Bryce," I say, "never speak to someone that way ever again—especially someone that you love. You are not a mean person, and I'm not going to stand by and let you become one."

Except what can I actually do? When you're living in a pond of algae, you turn green. It doesn't matter how often someone tells you to stop.

CHAPTER 20

When I've finally gotten Bryce and Aurora into bed—but not yet to sleep—I hear Frank's gruff voice from the living room over the noise of the TV. "Someone's here for you!"

He never calls me by name (I'm not actually sure that he knows my name), but who else could he be talking to?

I poke my head out of the bedroom.

"What's going on?" I hear Bryce call from bed.

"You were gonna tell us a 'tory!" Aurora says.

I don't see anyone at first, just Frank flopping back into his recliner with a grumble. And then, peeking around the corner with the washing machine, I see part of a face and a bit of pink hair.

Fuchsia?

"I'll tell you a story in just a bit," I call back over my

shoulder. "I promise." I quickly close the door to the bedroom behind me, cross the main room, and come around the corner to the entrance way. "What are you doing here?"

She shakes her head. She's wearing her jacket, which might be pink but was clearly designed for winter in Florida, and she looks completely frozen.

"Here." I grab my jacket from the pile of coats. "Put this on. Warm yourself up."

She slides down until she's sitting on the floor with her back to the washing machine and my jacket over her like a blanket. Her teeth are chattering.

I sit down across from her in the entryway, scooting Bryce's snow boots out of the way.

Fuchsia takes her hands out of her pockets and reveals an inhaler clutched in her fist. She takes two shots of it and then leans back against the washing machine. "I just feel like I'm going to explode or something."

"What? Because of the inhaler? Isn't it supposed to help?"

"The doctor said I should use it whenever I feel like my chest is tightening up. But that's like all the time right now. And the inhaler isn't making it go away."

"You should go to the hospital then." I tug at her wrist. "Why are you here?"

Fuchsia closes her eyes and bows her head. "Because nothing is going to get better unless I tell someone," she whispers.

What is she talking about?

"I couldn't tell you at school." Her voice is so quiet I can barely hear her. "You never know when a teacher is going to overhear you, and I've learned my lesson about *that*."

Why does she have to be *so dramatic*?

I'm about to stand up and tell her that I'm done. That I'm done with her and all of her games. Just *done*.

But then she starts talking. "I threatened Crystal that I would call DCF if she made me move in with Michael. And then, I guess, Crystal told Michael because the next day he showed up to pick me up from school instead of my mom. And as soon as I got into his car he told me that if I ever pull something like that again, then I wouldn't live to . . . " Her voice cracks.

"Oh my gosh." My hand flies to my mouth. "Did he . . . Was he the one in the parking lot who . . . "

She squeezes her eyes shut. "I thought he was going to kill me. He was pointing the gun right at me before he shifted to the side and shot through the window of the car instead.

That sound of glass shattering. I can hear it so perfectly.

"He fired twice more just for fun. And then, like nothing had happened, he drove us out of the parking lot. Like nothing had happened!"

It was the day after that when Fuchsia kept going on and on about her asthma and about how she couldn't breathe—and I was getting annoyed with her!

"I'm so sorry." I reach out and awkwardly pull her into a hug.

When Fuchsia pulls away she shakes her head. "Who does that? I mean, really!"

All I can see is Lenny, who grew up with Frank for a dad and just spent four years carrying around bags of smelly old-people diapers for a living.

Fuchsia doesn't wait for an answer, though. She produces a makeup mirror from her pocket and checks her eyeliner.

"Have you told the police anything?" I ask.

"No," she says. "What good would that do?"

"Well, they can arrest him, can't they?"

"Yeah, and then one of his buddies will post bail for him, and I'll be dead before the trial even starts." She snaps the makeup mirror shut. "I feel better now that I told you, though. Thanks." She stands up.

"Where are you going?" I ask.

"Back to the apartment. We've got one more day there and then my mom's borrowing someone's truck so we can move our stuff to Michael's lovely place."

"Aren't you going to tell your mom? You can still call DCF. You do have a choice."

She stares at the floor. "I've learned my lesson about fighting back."

Her teeth are still chattering from the cold. I look away and swallow the lump in my throat back down. "Are you walking?"

"I walked all the way here, didn't I?"

"Yeah, well, I walked here from downtown earlier today. That doesn't mean I want to do it a second time."

"It's fine."

I look out the window. The driveway is empty, which means Lenny and my mom drove rather than hitching a ride from someone else.

Certain things are okay to spend gas on.

Even if the car were there, what would I do? Convince Frank to get out of his recliner? Force Fuchsia to get in the car with him? Try to reach the pedals myself and get pulled over immediately?

"Are you sure?" I say.

Fuchsia sticks one hand in the pocket of her pink Florida jacket and grabs hold of the doorknob with the other. "Time by myself will be good." She pauses and looks at me. "I really feel better, though. Thanks."

I pick my jacket up off the floor. "At least put this on. Your jacket couldn't keep anyone warm."

"Then what are you going to wear?"

"I'm not walking across town in the wind right now, so it doesn't matter."

Fuchsia purses her lips, but then she takes my jacket. "Thanks. I'll give it back to you tomorrow."

I nod. "I know."

And then I watch her walk out into the darkness, all alone, with the wind blowing hard.

One jacket isn't enough.

When I go back into the bedroom, Bryce and Aurora are still awake.

"Time for our 'tory!" Aurora cries, flinging Petunia the Sea Turtle clear across the room.

"Make it about two kids having to stop an evil mastermind this time," Bryce says, climbing onto the bed. "With lasers and car racing."

I crawl into their bed. It isn't simple like that. One evil mastermind that you can stop to make everything okay. Instead it's like a horrible disease that's found its way into every corner, one that's super contagious.

Aurora gets nose-to-nose with me. "'Tart the 'tory!"

I close my eyes. I can't.

"And it should have sleds with blaster rockets and ants that have magical powers," Bryce says.

"Zoey," yells Aurora. "You can't go to seep! You pomised a 'tory!"

But I can't. If I open my eyes I'll see Bryce and think of

Lenny and now flippin' Michael, too. My friend came to me to tell me that someone shot at her, and all I could do was give her a jacket.

This disease is everywhere, and it's like the only medical equipment I have to fight back with is a Q-tip.

"That's not fair," Bryce says. "You promised us. You can't go to sleep. It's not fair!"

Nothing's fair. Getting shot at means you're too scared to tell the police. Getting bullied by your boyfriend means you slap your daughter when she tries to stand up for you.

"Come on!" Bryce jostles me.

It's good for them to learn now that nothing's fair. Well, they've already learned that plenty of other places, but I might as well show them that it's true everywhere.

Aurora starts crying and flings herself on top of me. "Wake up!"

Bryce is down at the foot of the bed whacking at my ankles with his foam lightsaber. "Not fair! Not fair! Not fair!"

But I keep my eyes closed.

Eventually, they tire out and fall asleep. When they do, I slither out of their bed and head to the living room to watch angry news guys with Frank.

Because what's the point? Octopuses have three hearts, and all of mine have broken.

CHAPTER 21

In the morning on my way out the door, I see Silas disappearing around the corner, walking the same death march as yesterday.

"Wait," I yell. "Silas!"

Before I can think twice about it I'm charging down the road after him. I'm just wearing a thin hoodie since I don't have my jacket, and the frigid air grabs tight to me as I run. I get why Fuchsia didn't speak up at school about what happened, but still . . . "Silas!" I call again as soon as I turn the corner. I can't tell if he can't hear me or if he's ignoring me, but he doesn't turn around.

I keep running and zero in on that camo trucker hat. If he doesn't turn around, if he refuses to talk to me, I'll just barrel right into him.

I'm closing in. "Silas!"

He turns, but his face is that expressionless wall.

I stop right in front of him, and before I can even catch my breath I blurt out, "You didn't have anything to do with that shooting in the parking lot."

His face doesn't shift.

I let out a long breath. "Right, well," I mutter. "You probably already knew that, but I just wanted you to know that I know, too."

Silas squeezes his eyes shut. I watch him. Did he even hear me? Is he too closed off to care? Then, after a long moment, I see something.

A tear escaping from one of his squeezed shut eyes.

I look away. But then I look back because I don't want him to think that I think it's bad for him to cry.

I take another step toward him and bite my lip. "Kids suck," I whisper. "I don't blame you for going all mute mode on everyone."

He wipes the tear away and stares down at the sidewalk. "My dad had to hide the phone in the closet so I wouldn't hear it keep ringing. The crank calling started right after that shooting happened and they haven't stopped yet. He keeps playing my favorite music super loud, so I won't hear it." Then, he looks at me. Like *looks* at me. "But I shouldn't have stopped talking to you. You're not like the rest of them."

I don't say anything—mostly because I'm embarrassed how close I came to starting to think like the rest of them.

When we get on the bus, Silas takes his normal seat. This time, though, I don't sit across from him. I sit right next to him. He doesn't say anything, but he moves his backpack onto his lap to make room, so I know it's okay.

Sometimes if you don't have a jacket and you're sitting next to someone who does, you feel colder. But sometimes, if the right person is wearing it, you feel warmer.

The problem is that even if I now know that Silas didn't have anything to do with the shooting, that doesn't change what other people think.

Moments after we get off the bus, Brendan Farley walks by Silas and mutters, "Not in jail yet?"

What am I supposed to do? Shout: "It wasn't him!" Only to have him say: "How do you know?" and I say: "I can't tell you." I might as well be waving my tiny Q-tip around at the same time.

Someone like Matt could get away with that. Me? Not so much. Especially since Brendan has turned to me and is looking me up and down like I might as well be arrested, too.

Fuchsia has my jacket for me when I get to my locker. "You must have been cold this morning," she says. "Thanks for this."

I shrug. "There are worse things." I stuff the jacket into my locker and then look at her. "I think you need to tell your mom."

Fuchsia doesn't look up from a spot on the floor that she's staring at. "I've thought about it." She pauses. "But she would side with him. And I don't think I could handle that."

I open my mouth but then close it again. What can I possibly say? Because I know exactly what she means.

In homeroom everyone is all in a tizzy because today was supposed to be the last day that you could order valentine carnations, but Mr. Bontaff accidentally turned in our homeroom's envelope early.

Mr. Bontaff is hunched at his desk doing attendance, while a mob of mostly girls crowds around his desk, almost like they're threatening to lift him out of his chair and hurl him all the way to the faculty room to fetch that form back again.

"We'd already ordered twenty-eight flowers," Mr. Bontaff says without looking up from his computer. "That's more than one per person in this homeroom. Just divide them up when the order comes in."

"But I have seven best friends who all sit at my lunch table with me," wails Savannah Bobbins. "I need to give all of them a special carnation!"

"You can't make me choose between my best friends and my *boyfriend*, Mr. Bontaff." Taylor Dixwell says "boyfriend" loud enough to take down the walls. She and Andy Cardinelli were basically the first people to start being girlfriend-boyfriend in a serious middle school way, and she doesn't let anyone forget it.

Matt, as the new seventh grade student council president, takes charge. "Mr. Bontaff, can't you understand what we're saying? All we need is for you to go get the envelope back. I can even do it for you. Did you turn it in to Ms. Holmes? Because I can go to her room right now and get it back from her."

Mr. Bontaff shrugs. "Whatever you want."

Matt takes off like he's got a cape flying behind him and a giant *S* for Seventh Grade Student Council President emblazoned on his shirt.

The rest of the kids practically swoon back into their chairs.

"At least Matt's going to take care of it."

"Thank goodness."

"Can you imagine having to just split up the carnations that were already ordered? I've never heard of anything so unfair."

"Ugh, that'd be the worst thing ever."

A few minutes later Matt proudly comes back into the room holding aloft the envelope. "Ms. Holmes is even out sick today, but the sub and I managed to find this on her desk!"

I watch as kids crowd around Matt and the envelope waving their money, but all I can hear is those three words: *worst thing ever.* Kind of like how not getting to share your Mars colonization idea is *so unfair.*

Because that's the difference, isn't it? For them it's like an easy life is automatic, and when it's not, they're all ready to pour on righteous anger and think they can do something about it.

Probably because they're armed with more than a measly Q-tip.

I picture myself with that imaginary Q-tip. Honestly, what else do I have going to bat for me?

And then Ms. Rochambeau's words burble up from inside me against my will.

Suck it up.

CHAPTER 22

I manage to avoid Ms. Rochambeau for almost the whole day. Because what am I going to say when she asks me why I ran away before the mock debate yesterday? Lie and say my stomach hurt, but that, yeah, I was still able to walk all the way across town?

Social studies is my last class of the day, and I purposefully slip into my seat right before it starts when Ms. Rochambeau is busy answering questions from that girl who keeps getting 97s on things and wants to get 100s. And when I see her starting to zero in on me toward the end of class, I quickly stand up, mumble something about needing to go to the bathroom, and sign myself out before she can reach me.

There are ten minutes left to class, but I can totally stay in a bathroom stall for ten minutes.

I slip into the stall that has *you're a slut* carved on the side. I used to like to look at it sideways and pretend that it says *you're a slug* and that it was carved by a cockroach who was just trying to help his slug friend who was having some identity issues.

I hear two girls come in and then another one join them soon afterwards. None of them even use the toilet—one of those prearranged meetings. They're talking about the Valentine's Day carnations, of course.

"I sneaked a peek at our homeroom's form, and Jeffrey ordered just one carnation. Who's he going to give it to?"

"Ooh, I don't know. He was sick for the last dance, so we don't know anything really about who he likes."

"Maybe it's Nellie. I saw him watching her when she was giving her book report in English and he looked more interested than he should have."

"I don't know. Remember how he moved out of the way to let you get ketchup during lunch yesterday? What if it's you that he likes?"

The second lets out an excited squeak like a giddy hamster. "Do you think he could?"

The first girl squeaks back. "Maybe that one carnation is for you!"

"Ooh eee!" the third girl exclaims.

I can hear them jumping around together.

Suck it up totally means hide in the bathroom and listen to a hamster mosh pit, right?

Finally, they leave, and I exhale. I get what Fuchsia said yesterday about needing to be alone. The only problem is it feels good for the first two seconds, but by the third second, all I can think is:

I'm all alone.

Except when I hear a noise in the stall next to me and suddenly realize that I'm not.

It's like a muffled sob. How long has someone been in there?

I peek underneath the stall. The other girl is wearing pink sneakers. Specifically Fuchsia's pink sneakers.

"Fuchsia?" I say.

No response.

"Are you okay?"

Another muffled sob.

I push open my stall door and come around to knock on hers. "Are you okay?"

I hear her slide the lock out of the way, and the door swings open to reveal a puffy, tear-stained Fuchsia.

"No," she sobs. "I'm not."

It's been years since I've seen Fuchsia cry. She was stone-faced when she was taken from her mom after that rainy day in second grade. And since then she'd get pulled from one foster family and plunked down in another, but did she ever cry? Did she ever do anything except roll her eyes and sigh and act like the world was just giving her a headache?

But here she is sitting on a toilet with tears pouring down

her face like that outer shell of a person has been kicked aside and all that's left are her quivering, crumpled-up insides.

I squeeze right into the stall and wrap her up in a hug. A good one. Like the ones that Connor sometimes gives me.

Her chest is shuddering against me, and I keep holding her tight.

"I'm just so scared," she finally whispers into my shoulder.

"Are you scared of Michael?"

She gulps in air and pulls away from the hug to look at me. "It's not just that. I was thinking about how you said I had a choice. Well, let's pretend I somehow find the courage to actually call DCF—and it's the wrong thing to do?"

The hair around her face is matted with tears, and I use my finger to gently comb some of it back behind her ear.

"I know what foster care can be like," she continues. "It wasn't that bad for me when I was in it, but it could have been so much worse. And what if I go back and it's a nightmare, and the whole time all I can think is: 'I did this to myself.'"

Her eyes are so scared, and I have no idea what to say. I pull her back into a hug.

"I always thought I hated having random people in control of my life." Her words are muffled against my shoulder. "But it's like I need that. I don't want it up to me. I don't care who it is, I just want someone to decide."

The bell rings, but I don't stop hugging her. I can walk all the way home if I have to.

"It's just too hard," she cries.

"But," I finally whisper, "that doesn't mean that you don't know the right thing to do."

Fuchsia pulls away and rubs her forehead. "Yeah, the right thing to do means getting my mom so mad that she'll never forgive me and pissing off an angry guy with a gun." She closes her eyes. "I've even memorized the DCF person's phone number. I just have to be brave enough to call it." She opens her eyes and looks up at the ceiling. "And I'm not."

I stare at her, at her eyeliner-streaked face and her swollen eyes. Why should anyone have to be that brave?

"Okay," Fuchsia finally says, standing up. "My mom's probably waiting for me outside. I've got to go."

"Is there something I can do to help?"

She shakes her head.

At least I can help her clean up her face before she leaves the bathroom. The eyeliner streaks are damp enough that a paper towel wipes them away. It's been awhile since I've seen Fuchsia without makeup, though, and suddenly I feel like I'm looking at her second grade self again.

I didn't really know how to help back then, and I'm not sure I know any better now.

Fuchsia doesn't want company when she heads out to the parking lot—and since, when we pass by the doors next to the locker room, I can see her mom's car waiting there for her in the space where the buses had been, I don't argue. I didn't really have a choice, but it sure would have been a good day to catch the bus rather than having to walk home again. My feet still haven't forgiven me for turning them into chunks of ice.

As I pass the entrance to the library, I peek inside. The two music stands are set up again for a mock debate. An eighth grade boy is already at one and standing at the other is Matt Hubbard.

I tuck myself behind the giant cardboard cutout of Harry Potter saying, "Read!" that Mr. Herd has set up on the side of the entrance.

"Guns are used exclusively for killing," Matt is saying, "and why should we trust people with that ability when clearly the statistics show that people cannot be trusted?" His voice is so confident. Like he couldn't possibly be wrong. After he goes through all the horrible statistics he copied into his notebook, he finishes with a triumphant, "Guns are evil, and that's why we should take the steps needed to make our society safer and outlaw them completely."

"And wouldn't that be wonderful," the eighth grader starts in, "for all law-abiding citizens to be unarmed and defenseless at the mercy of *criminals*, who, by the way, don't follow laws and will have all the guns they want." He's reading from his notebook, too, like he did the same thing as Lydia and copied down NRA talking points word for word. "No, ladies and gentlemen, the answer is not outlawing guns. Instead, we need to be eliminating gun-free zones where innocent people can be picked off like pigeons on a power line. We don't need fewer guns. We need more guns in the hands of more people. Only that will make us safe."

"Not if those people are bullies." The words came out of my mouth, and not in a whisper either, but in a shout loud enough to get the whole debate club to turn and look at me. I've knocked over the friendly Harry Potter cardboard cutout, but I can't get myself to pick it up, mumble "Sorry," and run from the room.

There is too much inside me that's screaming. That eighth grader might not believe that stuff, but Frank does. And we deserve better than having everything decided by people like Matt and people like Frank. What about everyone in the middle?

"What do you think should happen when a kid is threatened by a grown-up with a gun?" I say, taking a step forward. "Is she supposed to whip out her own and kill him? Because that's the kind of decision she needs weighing on her, right?" I turn to face Matt Hubbard, and I don't care that he has nice brown eyes. "Has it ever occurred to you that maybe guns aren't evil and that most of the people who own them aren't evil either? You're all so happy to decide Silas Fletcher is a monster just because he wears camo. Can you even fit into your brain the possibility that he's actually one of the most interesting people that goes to this school? And am I a monster, too, just because I have a camo jacket? Are you happy to imagine the drool dripping off my monster jaws? Do you want to pretend I ate a whole bunch of BABIES for BREAKFAST?"

Matt's mouth has dropped open, and the eighth grade boy is looking at me like I just beamed in from space. I can see Lydia peering from behind him, trying to see better, her eyes wide.

"You need to wake up!" I'm really shouting now. "We're not living in some sort of black-and-white pretend world. You act like it has to be all or nothing, like it's some kind of game. But there are actual people dealing with this. Actual people who have to say goodbye to their kittens. Actual people who have to hide their phones in the closet. And it's not a game to them!"

"Zoey," I hear Ms. Rochambeau say. "I'm so—"

But I don't hear what she says next because I'm setting the Harry Potter cutout back upright and running out the door.

I didn't mumble sorry. It probably wouldn't have made much difference at that point.

Since I totally just told off Matt Hubbard and some eighth grade boy.

I stop running when I reach the sidewalk. I look up at the sky. I don't know if anything I said made sense, but somewhere between the gray sidewalk and the gray sky, a laugh burbles out of me.

And it's such a loud laugh against that gray sky.

I can see the headlines: *Zoey Albro Delivers an Unhinged But Epic Smackdown to Two Confused Boys Who Thought They Were Better Than Her.*

It's been so long since I laughed, and it feels amazing. Like there's a whole big beautiful open ocean of freedom inside me. A tear drips down my cheek. A laughter tear. Not that other kind.

Who's clueless *now*?

I start walking, but I don't feel the cold like I did yesterday. It's like releasing all those words set off fireworks inside me, and they're still exploding all warm and bright.

How on earth did I do that?

And then I realize: Matt and that boy were just two screaming monkeys.

And I've had plenty of practice with those.

CHAPTER 23

Now that I know how long it takes me to walk home, me and my warm, fireworks-exploding insides decide I can take a short detour up toward Route 14 where Family Services is. Because there's a question I need them to answer.

I find the office in a building that used to be a house. The front part is an insurance company, but a sign leads me around back. Once inside, I go up a few stairs to find a room with three desks squeezed in, surrounded by big happy posters of kids.

The woman at the closest desk looks up. "Hi. How can I help you?"

"Hi . . . um . . . I just wanted to make sure that my family is all up to date. You know, with the forms we need to file for electricity help."

"Did your power go off?"

"Oh, it's on now. I just wanted to make sure that last form we filed was all correct."

She turns to her computer. "It probably was if your power is on, but let me pull up your records."

I give her my address and then wait, shifting between my feet as I stare at a poster offering free tax help to qualifying families.

Maybe someday our family won't "qualify" for everything.

"Yup, it looks like your form was turned in about a month ago, and that it was all filled out correctly."

"Who turned in the form? Does it say?"

"A Kara Albro. Is she your mom?"

It's like another burst of fireworks has gone off inside me.

"She sure is," I say.

I don't walk the rest of the way home—I run.

When I get there, Frank is in his usual spot, but now Lenny is also there, sitting on the couch surrounded by classifieds with the phone cradled between his shoulder and his ear. "Are you still looking for someone to do deliveries?" he asks. "Nope. Okay then." He hangs up, swears, and then starts dialing the next number.

My mom is home, too, since Friday nights are the best tip night and always go to the more senior waitstaff. I watch her in the kitchen as she works on getting Hector's formula ready. "Mom, I need to talk to you."

"Can't right now, Zoey." She starts shaking the bottle of formula. "Maybe later."

Lenny stands up to announce he's leaving to go fill out an application for a maintenance late shift at the hospital.

"Good luck, sweetheart!" my mom calls after him.

I hand my mom the nipple for the bottle that she's looking for. "We need to talk now, Mom."

She tests out the temperature of the formula on the back of her hand, and then goes over to scoop up Hector from his ExerSaucer. She thinks she can ignore me.

But I'm not going to let her.

"Here," I say, picking up the bottle from the counter. "Let me feed Hector."

She squints at me and then releases him to my outstretched arms.

I cradle Hector in one arm and give him the bottle with the other, just like my mom does. "Now," I say, "we can talk in your bedroom, or we can do it right here." I gesture to the back of Frank's balding head. "But we need to talk."

My mom glares at me. "I told you *no*."

"But this isn't just about you," I say, raising my voice. "This is about me, too. And Bryce and Aurora and Hector. If you still claim to be our mom then you better—"

"Fine!" she hisses. "But keep your voice down." She spins around and walks into her bedroom, and I follow after her.

As soon as I close the door behind us, I turn to face her. "Lenny doesn't treat you right."

"You've got a lot of nerve bringing this up again," she says, her eyes narrowing.

"But you need to explain something to me that I don't understand." I step toward her. "Why didn't you tell me the truth? You *knew* that Lenny never turned in that form to the power companies. You knew it wasn't your fault and that the form hadn't been filled out wrong, because otherwise you wouldn't have gone and filled out another one and turned it in yourself!"

My mom glares at me and then looks away. "I just figured it was worth a try."

"Did you even tell Lenny you'd filled it out fine? Does he even know how the power came back on?"

"The main thing is we have power."

"But it's not fair that he blamed you for that and that now he's blaming you for why he lost his job. It's not fair!"

She shakes her head. "I should have been paying attention to the gas gauge. I was so focused on getting that ground beef. I thought that it was going to fix things, but I just screwed things up more."

This is where I need to come up with my rebuttal, but not by discrediting my opponent. I need to do the opposite. "Mom, you didn't—"

"My job is to take care of you," she says without looking up. "And I am doing the best I can to make this work. This is our shot at a good life. With a stable place to live, that has heat and electricity and a kitchen with enough to eat."

"But Lenny isn't—"

"He's just upset about losing his job. It'll be better once he gets back on his feet. And, look, he's filling out a job application right now. He's doing the right things."

The right things? "Mom, he made it sound like you were the reason he lost his job. That's ridiculous."

But it's like she doesn't even hear me. "I shouldn't have cried. That always makes things worse. I just need to make sure I'm thinking through things first, so I don't screw up like I did with the gas tank. And make sure that I'm thinking clearly in the grocery store. And do a better job of . . ."

Suddenly I see my old mom, the waitressing mom. Thinking, thinking, thinking. Planning every little detail. Except that this time the customer she's waiting on is sending back pizza after pizza and blaming her for it every time. She's doing everything she can to figure out some way to get the next pizza right.

And if you're just watching that from the other side of the room, all you'd see is one incompetent waitress.

When it's really the customer that's the problem.

"Mom, we can't live with him anymore."

"You can't be serious."

"We can find someplace. We did before, right?"

"With four kids now, and no security deposit saved up and

no car of our own. And don't forget that I wouldn't even have my job if it wasn't for Lenny. Restaurants don't hire waitresses who are missing teeth."

"So just because he bought you a new set of teeth, he owns you now?"

She looks away.

And I realize that's what my mom really thinks. Yes, he does.

"Mom, whatever you owed for your teeth has been paid off for a long time."

She shakes her head. "Not when I keep making mistakes all the time."

No matter how good a person's rebuttals are, nothing matters if the person is living in a whole different reality. It's Lenny who I need to discredit. Who needs to be held up so my mom can see how he really is. "But, Mom, don't you get it? It's not you making mistakes. It's not you at all. It's *him*! He's the one who didn't turn in the form. He's the one who yelled at one of the old folks and got himself fired. He's the reason Bryce is having nightmares every night. It's him!"

She looks at me. Likes she's really hearing me for the first time.

"It's not you, Mom," I repeat, quieter this time. "It's him."

My mom sinks down onto the edge of the bed. Her mouth is slightly open and her eyes are fixed straight ahead.

"Every night?"

I nod.

She shakes her head. Finally she murmurs, "He should get another chance."

"Are you serious?"

"Instead of automatically giving up and going back to the broken toilet apartment? Instead of giving up on my kids having a father figure? Instead of giving up on having a boyfriend who can hold a job and tells me that my cooking smells good? Yeah, he gets another shot."

"Mom, Bryce is starting to talk the same way as Lenny. Is Lenny really the kind of person you want him looking up to?

She purses her lips and closes her eyes.

Hector starts crying. I look down to see that his bottle of formula isn't tipped back enough for him to get the last drops. I quickly fix it, and he quiets down to start sucking again.

My mom opens her eyes. "You can't mention this to Bryce or Aurora. If they breathed one word of it to Lenny . . ." She bites her lip and shakes her head. "He should get another chance."

When Lenny comes back home, he's all upbeat. "Had a good chat with the manager, and I got the job!"

"That's great!" my mom says. She's in the kitchen, mixing up some meatloaf.

"Yeah, he was just a few years ahead of me back in high school. Knows a lot of the same people."

"Wow, Lenny, I'm so proud of you."

"And the pay is even better than it was at the nursing home."

Things are all flowers and sunshine for the rest of the evening. Lenny even takes the meatloaf out of the oven for my mom and tousles Bryce's hair when Bryce shows up to get his plate of meatloaf.

But I don't buy it. I don't believe in Lenny's good moods anymore.

After I've gotten Bryce and Aurora into bed and told them a story, my mom and Lenny are cuddled up together on the couch, watching the dancing on *Make It or Break It* like they used to. After a while Lenny heads for the bedroom, and my mom silently scoops up Hector from his ExerSaucer and follows behind.

My mom might have said I'd regret it for the rest of my life if I spied on them again. But I'm pretty sure I'll regret it more if I don't.

Frank is fiddling with his cigarette in his recliner during a commercial break, which is enough for me to start across the main room—crawling so there's no chance he'll notice me.

With my octopus eye in position, I look into their bedroom. My mom is changing Hector's diaper, while a still upbeat Lenny is pacing around, twirling a sock in his hand. "This is going to be great. I can't believe it's even more money than before. You'll have to switch your hours at the Pizza Pit, of course," he says. "I won't be able to eat during the shift at the hospital like I could at the nursing home, so I'm going to need to have a better dinner ready for me when I get home."

My mom looks up with a start. "But I can't just shift hours like that. Connor's been doing the lunch shift forever, and he can't change those hours because he works nights at the brewery. And Ricky wouldn't let me switch things anyway. If I say I can't work nights, then he'll say I don't need to come back!"

Lenny plops down on the bed, lifts up one of his feet, and starts cleaning between his toes. "Well, you could just find another job. One where you don't have to deal with that Connor always poking his nose into our business."

My mom stretches the Velcro on the new diaper into place. "Are you serious?"

"Look. I'm not the one getting all worked up here," Lenny says. "You just need to go with the flow a little. I mean, it's just a job."

"It's my job."

He shrugs. "Like I said. Just a job. And considering the mess you've put us in, you better get your head screwed on straight soon." He finally looks up from his toes. "Now, where's that expensive smile of yours?"

My mom doesn't smile. She doesn't even look up. She's managed to stuff Hector into his pajamas, and one by one she's snapping them up.

Snap.

Snap.

Snap.

After she gets to the last one and moves Hector into his crib, she stands up straight—and then walks out of the room.

She blows past me and heads right into the bathroom. I scramble off the washing machine and knock on the door.

"Mom," I whisper. "It's me." Without waiting for an answer I slip inside the door and shut it behind me. My mom is sitting on the floor against the wall, her head buried in her knees.

"I told you you'd regret it if you spied on us again," she says. "You shouldn't see me like this."

I don't say anything. I just slide down next to her.

"I don't know what to do," she whispers. "I always thought I just had to explain myself better. That if I could do that, he'd understand." She looks up, tears streaming down her face. "But I don't think it matters what I say. I don't think he cares one bit about understanding me."

"I don't think he does either," I say. I stare at Lenny's perfectly lined-up shaving items: his shaving brush, his tub of shaving cream, his lather bowl, his razor—always lined up by size, with the handle of the razor perfectly parallel to the wall. "And I know that you said that he doesn't hit you, but that doesn't matter. He's still making sure that you're scared."

My mom reaches for a towel and wipes her face. I picture Fuchsia with the lines of eye makeup running down her cheeks. There are too many people hiding in bathrooms.

"It was Fuchsia," I blurt out.

My mom turns to me. "What was? What are you talking about?"

"The shots that were fired in the parking lot. That was Crystal's new boyfriend trying to scare Fuchsia."

"Oh, Fuchsia." My mom closes her eyes and buries her face back in the towel. When she emerges again, she takes a deep breath. "That whole family is trouble."

I eye the rest of Lenny's perfectly folded bath towels. But not us, right?

She stands up and tries to put the towel back the way he had it.

"What are you going to do about Lenny?" I ask.

She shakes her head. "I can't lose my job."

"What if we were able to find our own apartment?" I whisper.

"I told you. I don't have enough saved up to pay a security deposit."

"But if we just tried?"

She bows her head and closes her eyes. "He can't know."

I don't take my eyes from his perfectly square towels. "We won't let him find out."

CHAPTER 24

On Saturday morning, my mom announces that she's going grocery shopping. "Who wants to come?" she says, staring directly at me.

I nod. "I'll get Bryce and Aurora ready."

I drag Bryce and Aurora out of their pajamas with the promise that we can hang out in the toy aisle as long as they want, and finally the two of them along with Hector are strapped into the back seat of Lenny's car.

And I realize how impossible this all is without our own car. If we leave, what's that going to look like? Us walking down the shoulder of the road hauling a car seat and a booster seat with us?

My mom takes the road that leads up to Route 14. I hate the way my mom drives these days. Every time she steps on the accelerator it's so tentative. It's like she's scared she's going to use too much of Lenny's gas.

"Why are we going this way?" Bryce calls from the back.

"We're going to the J & H Supermarket this time," my mom says, without taking her eyes off the road.

"But, that one doesn't have the cart with the steering wheels," he whines.

"They're having a sale," my mom says without batting an eye, "on ground beef."

Part of me wonders if she's lost her mind, but then when she pulls into the parking space, she hands me the EBT card. "Don't spend more than five bucks and don't buy anything except for ground beef. And keep the kids occupied as long as you can. I'll meet you back here."

She gets out, hoists Hector onto her hip, and starts walking quickly out of the parking lot—toward Family Services.

Half an hour later, Bryce and Aurora are driving packages of Matchbox cars around in the toy aisle when my mom shows up again. She shakes her head when I meet her eyes. "Not a single opening for low-income housing," she whispers. "The waiting list is years long."

"We'll find something," I say. "Right?"

She watches Bryce and Aurora as they scoot around with their cardboard boxes yelling, "Zoom!" "Wherever we end up," she says, "we're going to need a car and there's no way we can afford one right now."

"But we can walk places. If we lived downtown, we'd be close to the laundromat, and you'd just have a long walk to work instead of the other way around," I say.

"With Hector? And then you walk all the way back with him and Bryce and Aurora after you pick them all up? There's no way."

I don't know what to say. How is it possible to have no visible cage around you, but to be so trapped?

My mom bites her lip. "But Lenny is going to expect me to either ask for new shifts when I go in to work today—or to quit. And I won't. I can't!"

Bryce crashes his Matchbox car box into a display of Valentine's Day decorations, and they all go flying.

"Bryce, quit it!" my mom yells, and both of us are soon on our knees picking up packages of paper plates and paper cups covered in hearts and containers of heart confetti.

"We'll find something," I whisper to her. There's no other option.

I pick up the last bunch of items on the floor, hot pink headbands with bobbly hearts. They're practically screaming Fuchsia's name, and I'm tempted to jam one into my jacket pocket, but my mom's too close and might see me.

Nothing in life is fair. We shouldn't be forced to choose between a place to live and life with Lenny, and if Fuchsia is going to get threatened by an angry guy with a gun, she sure deserves to have a hot pink headband with bobbly hearts. Except that she doesn't have a friend with enough money to buy it for her.

On our walk back to the car, my mom pulls me close to her and shows me a little scrap of paper with a phone number.

"What is that?" I ask.

"I got it from a poster at Family Services." She pauses. "It's a domestic violence hotline number."

"Are you going to call it?"

"I don't know. Do you think I should? He's never hit me."

"Mom. You're scared. I'm scared. That counts."

She bites her lip. "But . . . what if . . ."

I stop walking and look at her. "What if they can help us find a place to stay? You need to call them. I'll get the kids in the car while you do."

A tear slips down onto her cheek, but she nods. "Okay."

When I've gotten Bryce, Aurora, and Hector all buckled in and kept them occupied by singing "Baby Beluga" about forty times in a row, my mom climbs into the driver's seat and stows her phone in her purse.

"So?" I ask.

"We need to have a safety plan in place if we ever manage to leave," she whispers. "And we can apply for a protective order so Lenny has to stay away from us. They asked if he cares about his reputation enough to obey a protective order." She lets out a long breath. "I think that he does."

Behind me, the back seat is full of shout-singing about baby belugas in the deep blue sea. "Did they know of a place for us to go?" I ask.

She shakes her head. "The shelter is full right now."

"So, the protective order can work, but only if we can actually find a way to leave."

My mom sighs and starts the engine. "Yup."

When she pulls out of the parking lot, I turn to her. "What made you change your mind?"

"About what?"

"About Lenny." I'm tempted to mention the whole slapping thing, but I want her to answer the question.

She bites her lip. "I think I've known deep down for a long time, like a creeping feeling of numbness getting bigger every day. But it was just too unbearable to think about. Especially when I couldn't see any way out." She looks over at me. "It was when Lenny talked to you the way he talks to me. When he refused to believe you about that debate club of yours and said you just wanted to make trouble." She shakes her head and looks back at the road. "That was when it started to click for me."

Even though what he said to me was nothing compared to

what he's said to her. How is it so different when you're the one who's being bullied?

I stare out the window at the fancy grocery store and car dealerships that we're driving past. Tied to the new cars are balloons bouncing around at the mercy of the wind.

"Will you drop me off downtown on the way home?" I ask. "I think I need to see Fuchsia."

"Because we don't have enough going on already, right?"

I give my mom a look.

"Fine. I'll drop you off nearby," she says. "It would just be easier if problems happened one at a time."

When she pulls the car up to the falling-apart building downtown where Fuchsia lives, she leans over. "You know I can't waste any gas coming back to pick you up, right? The only way I could justify the trip to J & H Supermarket was the sale on beef."

"I know. I'll walk." Then I add, "It'll be good practice."

My mom rolls her eyes and shifts back into drive. "Right. As if we're ever going to make this happen."

The door to the building with Fuchsia's apartment is only partway closed, and I push through it and head up the rickety stairs. Someone at one point tried to paint half of the stairway bright green but then gave up. As though all this place needed was a new coat of paint to freshen it up.

I knock on the door to their apartment, and a few moments later I hear Fuchsia's voice. "Who is it?"

"It's me. Can you let me in?"

A lock is undone, and the door opens to reveal Fuchsia with her hair all squirrely like she's just gotten out of bed.

"What are you doing here?"

"Did I wake you up?" I ask as I step inside.

"Naw," she says, "but what's the point of getting out of bed?" She closes the door behind me.

"Where's your mom?"

She wraps her pink hoodie tighter around her. "Saturday morning shift at the bakery." She peers out the window through the slats in the broken blinds. "You know, I've decided to call that DCF person."

"You have?"

Fuchsia leans against the window frame. "Just haven't done it yet."

I nod. "I know you say you like your alone time, but I figured I should be here with you, whether or not you decide to call." I take my coat off and hang it over the one chair that's pushed to the side of the room. "Sometimes it's better to have someone at your side."

Fuchsia eyes me. "Thanks," she says slowly.

"How are you going to make the call?"

"What do you mean?"

"Like what phone are you going to use?"

"The lady across the hall lets me use her phone for emergencies," she mumbles—but she doesn't move.

"Oh," I say. The air in the apartment is cold, and I pull my coat back on.

"Are you going already?" Fuchsia asks.

I shake my head and sit down in the chair, tucking my hands underneath me. I stare at Fuchsia. Without her makeup on she looks about as scared as Aurora did when she was surrounded by all those honking cars.

I keep my voice low. "You know, you can get a protective order to keep someone away from you. You could get one against Michael."

"Yeah," Fuchsia smirks. "Then I can be all: 'Sorry, Crystal, I can't move in with him because then he'd have to be arrested.' That'd be hilarious except for the part where she'd kill me herself."

"But if you tell her about what Michael did?"

Fuchsia shakes her head. "She wouldn't believe me. She'd kick me out."

"Is that really any worse? You'd just end up calling the DCF lady after that."

She glares at me. "Yeah, it's worse. You want to try and convince me that it'd be fun to get kicked out by your mom?

To have her choose some angry troll-man over you? No. I'm going to be the one who gets to call the shots. Not her."

Fuchsia peers over the top of the hoary frost on the window pane to look outside and then goes to the fridge and pulls the door open. As soon as she does, a small ball of black-and-white fur zips in from the bedroom and starts weaving between Fuchsia's legs.

"Oh my gosh," I say. "Is that Jane Kitty?"

Fuchsia pulls out a quart of milk and closes the fridge behind her. "She can be totally asleep, but the sound of the fridge opening gets her every time." She pours a bit of milk onto a plate and places it on the floor.

Jane Kitty immediately starts lapping it up. "You and I aren't so different, are we, Jane Kitty?" Fuchsia says, stroking her little furry back. "And I'm going to lose you no matter what I—"

Fuchsia's voice cuts out early, and she turns away from me. She doesn't want me to see her cry again.

I take a deep breath. Maybe I can't give Fuchsia a bright pink headband, but that doesn't mean I can't help a different way. "What if I were here with you when you did it?" I ask. "If I were here when you told your mom about Michael?"

"You mean, so she can kick you out, too?"

"Sometimes people are different if someone else is there." I shift on my hands. "And, if she kicked us both out together, then you wouldn't be alone."

I expect Fuchsia to smirk and maybe throw something at me, but she doesn't.

"Okay," she whispers. She keeps petting Jane Kitty and doesn't look up at me.

"Did you say 'Okay'?" I ask. "Like you'll really tell your mom what happened?"

"If you're going to be here for it."

I watch as Jane Kitty finishes lapping up the milk and Fuchsia scoops her up into her arms. Fuchsia, who doesn't care if she has asthma, but is going to love that furry ball of kitten anyway.

Like how the cold air feels like nothing when you've just stood your ground and told off the whole debate club.

And how even the most organized trailer with nice curtains and a nice lamp and an alphabetized DVD collection is worth nothing if . . .

I stand up. "When's your mom going to be back?" I ask.

Fuchsia looks at the clock on the stove. "Probably an hour? I don't know—why?"

"The woman who lives across the hall. Do you think she'd let me use her phone, too?"

Fuchsia cocks an eyebrow at me. "She will if you tell her how much you love her birds."

"Her birds?"

"She's got like a hundred of them in there. Who do you need to call?"

I'm already halfway to the door. "I'll be right back."

As soon as I'm at the door to the neighbor lady's apartment, I hear the birds, and it only gets louder once I get inside. The neighbor lady is a bit old and stooped and has a small parrot hopping around on her shoulder with about another two dozen birds in cages behind her squawking up a storm, probably all arguing that they should get shoulder privileges, too.

"Just keep it short," she says over the racket of cheeps when I ask her if I can use her phone.

I follow her into another room, one that has even more birds.

"Your birds seem really sweet!" I say. Or enthusiastic.

The smell that hit me when she first opened the door into the apartment only gets stronger in the next room. I can't really place it. It's like damp newspapers but more funky. I'm pretty sure it's the smell of Too Much Bird.

Still, the little parrot hopping around on the neighbor lady's shoulder and burrowing its beak into its feathers is pretty cute. The lady grabs a little yarn ball from a pile on a small table as she passes it and tosses it up to the bird, who grabs it in its beak. Like a tiny dog with feathers.

The neighbor lady stops at the old-fashioned kind of phone. Not only is it the big kind that isn't a cell phone, but it's got a loopy spiral cord that's connected to the wall.

"Thank you," I say over the chirps.

I dial my mom's cell number.

"It's me," I say when she picks up.

"You better not be calling asking for a ride."

"I'm not."

"Good," she says. She drops her voice. "Because Lenny is already suspicious about why I had to drive all the way up to Route 14 for groceries. The ground beef sale calmed him down a bit, but he's still acting funny. It's like he knows!"

I cover my other ear to try to block out the bird sounds. I can barely hear her. "He doesn't know," I say.

"But I haven't told him yet that I would quit my job. He knows I haven't said that. I can tell. It's like he's watching me, waiting to strike. I know he's never hit me before but . . ."

"Where is he now?"

"He went over to Slider's to help him move a couch."

"Did they take the car?"

"No. Slider came by and picked him up, but I told you I'm not giving you a ride. I know he's going to check the mileage on the car as soon as he gets back, and I don't—"

"Mom," I cut in. "How much do you have saved up for rent?"

"Well, I didn't pay Lenny the rent I owe him yet, but that's the other thing—I think he knows about that, too. I told him I didn't have time to get to Walmart to cash this week's paycheck, but I've never been a good liar and—"

I try to ignore the panic in her voice. "Okay. So you have the money from this week's paycheck," I say. "That's something."

"And I still have a little bit left from my tips from the week but even then it all only adds up to one hundred and sixty-seven dollars."

"What if I was able to get someone to rent us an apartment for that much?"

"There's no way," she scoffs. "Rent for one hundred sixty-seven dollars? Have you lost your mind?"

"There'd just be one catch," I say.

"What? That it's a garbage can, not an apartment?"

"It just might come with people already living in it."

"Who?"

I take a deep breath. "Fuchsia," I say. "And maybe her mom if she wants to stay."

My mom sucks in her breath. "Oh, honey. You know what Crystal's like. Don't fool yourself into thinking she's changed."

"I know, Mom." I say. "But you know what happened to Fuchsia, and if that's happening to Fuchsia then what's happening to Crystal when no one's around to see?"

She's quiet for a long time, and all I can hear is the muffled cries of all the birds around me.

"It might be messy," I finally say, "but the only way we're going to have a chance is if we stick together."

CHAPTER 25

It took all the convincing I had to get my mom to put Hector, Bryce, and Aurora in Lenny's car and drive over to Fuchsia's apartment, so she can see the place and talk to Crystal. As soon as I open the door for Mom, she's at my ear whispering, "If he gets home before we do, I just know he's going to call the cops and tell them I stole his car." She shifts Hector onto her other hip. "And even if we do get back in time, he'll see the odometer. He'll know we went somewhere. What am I supposed to tell him?"

"Blame it on me," I say. "Tell him I was freaking out because my friend needed help and that it wouldn't have been right to ignore her."

My mom shakes her head. "As if that's going to be enough."

Bryce and Aurora have been standing in the doorway looking nervous. They know who Fuchsia is, but she's never been that nice to them. It's not like she's been particularly mean either, but she just hasn't been around little kids much. Even the foster families where she's stayed all had older kids, and it's like whenever little kids are around she gets itchy.

Which is one of the reasons why I just mentioned that maybe it could be good to have even more people around when she tells her mom—and why I haven't told her about my other idea yet. She's not necessarily going to be a fan.

Fuchsia pokes her head out of the bedroom, and I almost think she's about to slip back into it and pretend she never saw us, but then Jane Kitty zips out between her feet and leaps onto the windowsill.

"A kitty!" Aurora exclaims, forgetting all about how nervous she felt. She makes a beeline for the windowsill with Bryce right behind her, and soon you can't even see Jane Kitty because of all the pets and kisses being heaped onto her. Aurora isn't like other little kids that would yank a cat's tail, but she is going to get right in its face and tell it how "bootiful" it is.

I cross the room to where Fuchsia is watching her kitten get smothered in love.

"Aurora and Bryce will be really gentle," I say.

Fuchsia nods but she doesn't look convinced. "Remind me again why your whole family had to come?"

"My mom and I are just here to back you up when you

tell your mom about Michael—and . . . " I take in Bryce and
Aurora, who are still wearing their big puffy winter coats and
look like dirty Oompa Loompas. "And they just have to go
wherever we go."

When Crystal shows up twenty minutes later, she's pretty
surprised to find all of us here, too.

"What the—" she starts, but stops when she sees the little
kids.

"Come on," I whisper to Bryce and Aurora. "How about
you bring Jane Kitty to Fuchsia's bed in the other room and
keep playing there."

The magic of Jane Kitty means that they don't care where
they are, as long as they get to keep petting her head and rolling balls of tin foil at her belly for her to fend off like a spas-
tic ninja. When I come back out to the main room, my mom
and Crystal are staring at each other like they're in a full-on
showdown.

"I thought I told you I didn't need your pity," Crystal is
saying.

My mom crosses her arms. "I am not here because of some
pity party for you."

"Yeah, you with your great boyfriend and great place to
live. So, what are you here for then? Because I don't need you
to tell me you're better than me to know you think it."

My mom leans back against the wall. "I'm only here
because Zoey asked me to come."

Crystal's eyes find their way to me. I swallow. "Um . . . Fuchsia has something she needs to tell you."

"Does she?" Crystal drops her bag on the floor and comes around the table until she's inches away from Fuchsia. "And you needed witnesses for it, eh? It's that good?"

Fuchsia glares at the floor. "I don't have to tell you anything."

"Oh," tsks Crystal, "but what's the point of having an audience if you've got nothing to say? It seems like a real waste to—"

"Stop talking to her like that!" I blurt out. "You don't know what she's been through."

Crystal whips her head around. "Oh, really. And I should listen to you because you're her mother and you know what's best?"

"That's my daughter you're talking to," my mom says.

"Yeah, well she's in my apartment," Crystal snaps back.

"Not for long," Fuchsia says. Her voice is so quiet compared to her mom's. "Aren't we moving in with Michael this afternoon?"

"Yeah, well, this is still our apartment until that happens, and I'm not about to have—"

"Michael threatened me with his gun," Fuchsia says. Her voice is still just as quiet, but it stops her mom cold.

"What did you just say?" Crystal says.

"He fired it, too," Fuchsia says. "Not at me exactly, but not more than a foot away."

Crystal's voice has gone hoarse. "You're lying."

"I'm not."

"It's a lie, and you're a liar!" Crystal screams. "And I'm not going to stand here and—"

"You've been in Michael's car since Tuesday," Fuchsia says. "There's no way you could have missed the fact that his passenger door window isn't there anymore."

Crystal's face darkens. She opens her mouth, but no words come out. Instead, she just shakes her head.

The silence that follows is so complete that I can make out the frantic chirps from the birds in the apartment across the hall.

After a long, long minute, my mom speaks up. "If Michael has done that to Fuchsia, then it's pretty easy to imagine what kind of stuff he'd do to you. And I say that," she quickly adds when Crystal's eyes widen, "as someone who . . . " She takes a deep breath. "As someone who doesn't have a great boyfriend—at all."

Crystal sinks down into the chair, glares at my mom, and then looks away. "So, things are in the pits for you, and you want company, is that it?"

Crystal is like an unmovable rock. If the point of debate is to convince someone to see something in a new way, then it's time for us to bring it.

"What if you didn't have to move in with him?" I say.

"Because you're going to find a way to magically lower the rent? And why are you even here? This isn't your business."

I take a deep breath. "I know five people who are looking for a place to live who could help out with the rent."

Fuchsia cocks her head at me. "What? But you guys have that great trailer and . . .

"You can't be serious," Crystal says with a laugh. "Seven people in a one-bedroom apartment?"

I shrug. "Seven people and not a single one of them is an abuser."

"Seven people and one of them once called me a slut," Crystal shoots back.

"I never said that," my mom jumps in.

Crystal glares at my mom. "That isn't what your boyfriend told me."

My mom crosses her arms. "Well, he told me you called me a slut and a whore, so was he telling the truth about that? Because I'm pretty sure he was just trying to destroy the only real friendship I had."

"That was a friendship? Mostly I think it was you telling me what I should and shouldn't do—and this doesn't seem all that different."

When my mom just purses her lips without saying anything, Crystal stands up. "You all have lost your minds. And I don't know what you're talking about with that 'abuser' talk. I told Michael that we'd move in this afternoon, and I'm not going to go back on that."

"Because you're scared of him?" I say.

"You know that right now I'm shaking in my boots that I'm here," my mom says, "and that Lenny will see the gas mileage when he gets back and know I took his car."

Crystal looks at my mom, but she doesn't say anything. Finally, she looks away and mutters, "I'm not scared of him."

But I don't believe a word of it.

"You move in with Michael if you want," Fuchsia looks up at her mom from where she has tucked herself farther into the corner of the kitchen. "But I'm not going anywhere. And they should be able to stay here with me." She kicks at one of Bryce's boots that he left near the door. "Why not?"

"I'll call the police on you," Crystal says.

"That's fine." Fuchsia shrugs. "I'll have already called them about Michael. Zoey told me about protective orders, and I don't want that man allowed anywhere near me."

"You want them to take you back into foster care?" Crystal hisses.

"Then they do. But they wouldn't have to—not if you stayed here and called the police about Michael for me."

Crystal squeezes her hands together, and I realize that they're shaking.

My mom stands up and puts a scrap of paper on the table. "That's the domestic violence hotline number. You should think about calling it no matter what you decide about us."

Crystal's only answer is to glare at my mom and keep squeezing her hands together.

"Zoey, come on," my mom says. "I think it's time for us to go." She bangs on the bedroom door. "Bryce! Aurora!" she calls. "Let's go!"

She opens the door to reveal Bryce cupping Jane Kitty in his hands like the most precious jewel in the world. Aurora is wrapping Bryce's legs up in a bear hug like it's the only way to get out her need to squeeze something super tight with love.

"Oh, please," Bryce sobs. "Don't make us leave yet. This kitten loves us! And we love her!"

His voice is trembling, and there are tears in his eyes.

My mom pauses. And in that pause, I hear a voice.

Crystal's voice.

"You can stay. You can all stay." She's looking at Bryce as she lets out a long breath. "We'll make it work."

CHAPTER 26

"What do you mean 'All our stuff'?" Bryce calls from the back seat.

My mom doesn't take her eyes off the road. "We need to pack it up—and quickly. You can't ask too many questions."

"Are we going to use this car?" I ask.

My mom shakes her head. "Too risky. But Connor's already at the Pizza Pit for the lunch shift. I think he'd let us use his to get our stuff out of there." She grips the steering wheel hard. "As long as Lenny isn't already back home."

"So do you mean I have to pack up all my toys?" Bryce asks.

"That's what she means," I say.

"And Petunia?" Aurora asks. "Where Petunia going?"

I twist around in my seat. "We're all going to be staying together and Petunia is going to stay with us. It's just that we're going to be living in a new place."

Bryce has been scratching at the old sticker from school that's stuck to his shirt, but he stops and looks at me. "Where?"

I suck in my breath. "We're going to be living with Fuchsia and her mom in their apartment."

"WITH THE KITTY?!" Aurora shrieks. If she hadn't been buckled into her booster seat I think she would have rocketed clear across the car.

"Yes," I say, "with the kitty."

For the rest of the drive, all Bryce and Aurora can do is scream in excitement about the kitty. They only stop their shrieking when my mom pulls into the trailer park and slows down for each of our final turns.

The back seat is completely quiet when we pull into the parking spot next to the trailer—until I hear Bryce ask in a small voice. "Are Lenny and Frank going to move to the apartment with the kitty, too?"

"No," I say. "They're not."

"Oh, okay," he says.

"And you can't tell them that we're moving," my mom adds. "Okay? Not a word about this."

"So it's going to be a surprise for them?" Bryce asks.

"Yeah," she mutters, "something like that."

I'm right behind my mom when she walks up to the door to the trailer, and all I can think is *please-don't-be-home-yet, please-don't-be-home-yet.* My mom must be having the same thoughts because she's slowing down. It's like the door handle is covered with poison and she doesn't want to have anything to do with grabbing hold of it and opening the door.

"It's going to be okay," I whisper. "If Lenny's at home, just blame it on me. I wanted to take care of my friend."

My mom closes her eyes. "And we just wait for another day to pack up and move out." But then she sucks in her breath, and I realize she's holding back tears.

"It's going to be okay," I repeat. I wrap my arms around her just as firmly as she used to wrap her arms about me when she'd tell me things were going to be okay.

She bows her head, squeezing her eyes shut. "Now that I can see the way out, I want out," she whispers. "I just want *out!*"

I grab hold of the door handle. "We'll make sure that this is the last time we ever have to walk in this door." I push open the door and walk inside. All I can hear is the TV. Lenny and my mom's bedroom door is open, and I peek in. No Lenny.

Around the corner I find Frank in his recliner. "Has Lenny come back yet?" I ask over the noise of the TV.

"Does it look like he did?" Frank calls back without looking away from the TV.

I turn around to find my mom close behind me. "We need to go fast," I whisper.

She must be thinking the same thing because she turns on the spot, grabs a trash bag from the kitchen, and disappears into her bedroom.

"Come on, Bryce and Aurora! Let's go! We're going to clean up our room together, okay?"

Aurora practically skips into the bedroom, shouting, "It gonna be a soopize!"

I grab a couple more trash bags and head into the bedroom after her.

"Come on, Bryce!" I call. He's still trying to get his winter boots off without using his hands.

"Why do we have to hurry so much?" he asks when he finally appears at the door.

"We just do." I'm stuffing things into a bag at lightning speed. I pull the Mickey Mouse night-light out of the wall. "Think of it as a race."

"Petunia," Aurora is saying to her sea turtle, "we're gonna get to go live with a *kitty*!"

My mom pokes her head into our room. She's got Hector on her hip. "I'm going to run over to the Pizza Pit and borrow Connor's car." She's talking superfast. "As soon as I get back here with it, you've got to be ready to go. I'm going to leave Hector here with you. Can you get the car seats out of Lenny's car before then?"

I nod. "Okay. We'll be ready. Go!"

My mom looks at me for an instant and then sets down

Hector on the floor. "I'm going to leave my bag outside by the trash cans, but it's not trash." Then, she's gone.

Bryce starts play-fighting with the lightsaber and just barely misses Aurora.

"Bryce, put that down and start packing your things into this bag, okay?"

I finish throwing the rest of Aurora's clothes into a bag and start in on Bryce's to help him.

"Can we bring this lamp with us?" Bryce asks. "I really like this lamp."

"It's not ours, Bryce. I'm sorry." I grab clothes from off the floor. We'll figure out what's dirty later.

"But it's in our room," Bryce says.

I cram Bryce's sandals from last summer into the bag. Not that anyone can imagine wearing sandals when it's February. "I'm sure there's already a lamp at Fuchsia's apartment." When did he start liking that lamp?

I stand up, tie the two big bags shut, and pick up Hector. "I'm going to bring these outside and get the car seats ready. You put anything else that's ours in that last bag, and I'll be back in to get it in a few minutes."

Outside, Aurora's booster seat is easy to detach, but the base of Hector's big hulking car seat is a different story. It's like the release button on it is not an actual button but is instead just a different colored piece of plastic that has no intention of releasing anything and really wonders about why you keep punching it in the face. I'm still wrestling with the car seat when I hear my mom pull up at the curb. She better be able to get this thing out of here.

But when I finally extricate myself from the back seat and stand up, I see it's not my mom.

It's Lenny getting dropped off by Slider.

"Oh, hi!" I say. I can feel my hand instantly start to shake.

"What are you doing in my car?" he asks as Slider drives away.

I force a smile. "Just trying to fix Hector's car seat. It was getting too loose."

He sticks his head in the driver's side. He's looking at the odometer. "So where'd you go?"

"What do you mean?" I keep trying to jab at the car seat button because it's even harder when your hand won't stay still.

"Someone drove three point seven miles since I left. You know anything about that?"

"Oh, it was because of my friend. She was having a really rough time and I made my mom drive me over to see her."

Lenny raises an eyebrow at me. Maybe he does suspect something's up.

"Well, it was just three point seven miles, right?" I say. "I mean, she was having a really rough time."

"So you needed to pat her on the shoulder while she has some cry fest about a boy. Just don't use up my gas to do it."

Lenny is putting on his nice face for me but I can tell that underneath the gears are starting to turn.

He slams the car door shut and then looks back at me. "What's up with all those trash bags?"

"Oh. Those." I try to keep breathing. "We were doing a lot of cleaning . . . " But then I trail off—mostly because Bryce and Aurora have appeared on the stoop, and Bryce is still holding the lamp.

Lenny's nice face is gone. "What's going on?"

Aurora's eyes go all big. "IT'S A SOOPIZE! THERE'S A KITTY!"

He turns to me. "What's she talking about?"

"Oh, she's just really excited about cats these days," I say quickly. "I think she's starting to have an imaginary friend. Don't worry, there aren't any actual cats in the trailer."

Lenny turns to Bryce. "What are you doing with that lamp?"

"Um . . . " Bryce looks terrified. He puts it down on the stoop, like lamps always live on stoops. "Nothing."

Mom drives up to the curb in Connor's old Subaru, her face gray with fear. She comes to a stop, but the engine is still going.

"What in God's name is going on?" Lenny shouts.

Please don't drive off without us.

"We didn't want to leave the trash out in front of the trailer all week until the garbage truck comes," I say. I grab as many of the trash bags as I can, and hurl them into the trunk of Connor's car. "But we didn't want to put any more miles on your car, so my mom borrowed a car from someone else, so we could make a trip to the dump before it closes at five p.m." I walk back over to Lenny's car like I know what I'm doing, and even though everything inside me has turned to goo I jam my thumb into the car seat button like I mean it. It finally releases and lets me haul the car seat out of the car. With my other arm I grab Hector from where he's been playing on the back seat with a seat belt and head for Connor's car.

Lenny's face is shifting to a deep shade of red. "Whose car is that?"

"Let's go, Bryce and Aurora! We've got to go!" I call. "To the dump," I add, praying that they don't hear that part and decide not to come.

"WHOSE CAR IS THAT?" Lenny yells again, but he doesn't even wait for an answer. He's barreling up the stairs and into the trailer to see for himself what's inside—and what isn't.

Bryce and Aurora pile down the stairs right past him.

I pull open the back seat door, hurl in the car seat, pluck Hector into it, and thread the seat belt through it as quick as I can. I may be goo on the inside, but octopuses are basically made of goo and I've got all eight tentacles in motion. Aurora is suddenly filling the back seat with chants of "KITTYKITTYKITTYKITTY!" Bryce has thankfully left the lamp on the stoop and appears with Aurora's booster seat that I left lying on the ground.

I buckle them both in practically at the same time. I am a full-on octopus. I squeeze out the opposite door and climb into the passenger seat next to my mom who's still frozen at the wheel.

But as soon as I do I see Lenny coming toward us, gripping the lamp in one hand.

"*WHOSE CAR IS THAT?*"

My mom's knuckles are white from gripping the steering wheel.

His eyes. He's shaking.

But he's just a screaming monkey.

I put my hand on my mom's and squeeze. "Drive, Mom," I say. "Drive now."

And then just like she used to, my mom slams down on the accelerator, and we shoot down the road.

There's a muffled crash as the lamp is thrown right into the side of the car.

That wasn't our lamp anyway.

CHAPTER 27

Our first stop is the courthouse to file for the emergency pro-tective order. The process takes a long time—but when my mom calls Connor at the restaurant to see if he needs his car back I can hear him through the phone, insisting that we darn well better keep the car as long as we need it and that if we try to bring it back too soon he'll refuse to take the keys.

And then when my mom finally gets in front of the judge, he immediately issues the protective order.

Just like that.

My mom takes an extra copy of the paperwork she had to fill out, and the first thing she does when we get to Crystal's apartment is to put it down on the kitchen table. "You should do this, too. For you and for Fuchsia."

"Let's just remember that I'm the one who's letting you

stay in my apartment," Crystal says, glaring at my mom. "I
didn't say anything about letting you be the boss of me."

Still, when my mom's not looking I catch Crystal folding
up the forms and stowing them in the back pocket of her
jeans.

Fuchsia is out somewhere, but Jane Kitty is still around and
Aurora disappears into the bedroom after her. Bryce won't let
go of my leg. I keep rubbing his back.

My mom turns to me. "I'm going to drive Connor's car
back to the Pizza Pit and stay on for my dinner shift. Can
you . . ." She trails off and looks at Bryce.

"I'll get us all settled in," I say. "But can I have some money
so we can get something for dinner?"

My mom takes the stack of ones out of her pocket and
counts out five bucks for me. Then, she plunks a bunch of it
down on the table for Crystal. "For rent," she says.

Crystal counts it and then pockets it. "Better than nothing."

My mom hands me Hector and heads out, and I look up
to find Crystal eyeing me. "This place isn't baby-proofed, you
know," she says.

I nod. "I'll just watch him real well to make sure he doesn't
get into anything."

It's so awkward to still be standing near the door. But
there's only one chair and Crystal is sitting in it. And it's not
like I can move with Bryce suctioned onto me.

Was this really my idea?

Bryce tugs at my jeans and whispers, "Where are we going to sleep?"

I glance at Crystal. If she heard his question, she's not showing it.

"Well," I start, "it'll probably be more crowded than before."

Bryce looks around at our trash bags of stuff that are lined up in front of the sink.

And then he bursts into tears.

"Bryce . . ." I say. I detach him from my leg, so I can kneel down and wrap my free arm around him. Hector squirms out the other side of me, and even though I just said I would keep a close eye on him, I don't chase after him. Instead I wrap my other arm around Bryce, too. I don't even bother to ask him what's wrong, because what's the point? What *isn't* wrong?

Hector is crawling toward the radiator. He'll find out soon enough that it's hot, and he won't want to touch it again. Just don't start licking the lead paint. It's too bad we didn't have time to grab his ExerSaucer. There isn't much in the kitchen to distract him with.

Bryce is sobbing so hard that I feel his wet tears through my shirt, and I hug him harder. "I'm right here, Bryce," I whisper. "I'm always going to be right here."

Bryce's whole body shudders with sobs. His head is buried in my shoulder, and I try to rest my head on his, but instead he pulls away to look at me. "But it's—" He gulps with the force of a sob before he can say anything more. "But it's—" His eyes are so scared.

"But it's not here!" he finally cries, waving frantically at the three trash bags in a line. "The last trash bag. IT HAD MY LIGHTSABER IN IT!"

I close my eyes. "Oh, Bryce, I'm so sorry."

"And I need that lightsaber," he cries. "I need it! I need it! I need it!"

His buries his face back into me again.

"We'll find you another one," I murmur into his hair. "Don't worry."

I look around to see Hector sitting happily on the linoleum floor, playing with some take-out containers. Then another container is dropped right in front of him, and I realize Crystal has been washing them out in the sink and giving them to him. Her face is hard to read, but she doesn't look annoyed. More like curious.

"But I need it." Bryce is still whimpering into my shoulder. "I need it . . . " His chest shudders. "To fight off the bad guys."

My breath catches in my throat. I grab Bryce by the shoulders and hold him so I can see his face. "You don't need your lightsaber anymore. You're safe from bad guys here, okay? Do you understand me? You're safe."

Bryce is watching me with his puffy red eyes like he doesn't believe me.

"You're safe here," I repeat, and I pull him back into my chest.

And no one here is going to tell you not to cry when you're sad.

A few minutes later, Fuchsia comes through the door. She's a bit out of breath. "I found an extra mattress down in the basement, but I need help getting it up the stairs."

I release Bryce and follow Fuchsia down the stairs to help. I'm sure I'll get used these stairs.

"Zoey?"

I look up to see Bryce watching from the landing.

"Yeah?" I say.

"Did Fuchsia find that mattress just for us?"

"Yeah, buddy, I think she did."

Bryce bites his lip and nods—and then heads back into the apartment.

Fuchsia calls to me from the bottom of the stairs. "Zoey! Are you coming?"

"Yup! On my way!"

On Monday morning, I take the bus with Fuchsia. We don't talk much—she's never been much of a morning person and I haven't gotten much sleep, based on the fact that Bryce is still

waking up with nightmares, and when I try to get back to sleep
my mom and Hector are somehow always taking up most of
the bed. I guess the last time she and I shared a mattress with a
baby (that time it was Bryce), I was smaller.

It's weird that Fuchsia isn't waiting for me at my locker.
She had mumbled something about going to the nurse and
had disappeared as soon as we got into school. Maybe she
didn't sleep well the last two nights either. I don't know if she's
much of a fan of having to share a bed with Crystal, but she
insisted that Bryce and Aurora could use hers.

Still, it works out that she's not leaning against the locker
next to mine, since someone's decorated it up and down with
valentine hearts. I guess today is Valentine's Day. I stuff my
jacket into my locker and head into homeroom.

Inside, everyone's in a tizzy over who got carnations and
from whom and how many. Miss Popularity Savannah Bobbins
is at her desk surrounded by most of the homeroom. "Hold on!
I lost count again! I have to start all over."

I give them wide berth and find my way to a seat in the
back. As soon as I sit, I put my head down on my desk, and
close my eyes, but I can still hear her squealing.

"Who's this red one from?" someone says. "You know
what the red means, right?"

"Hey," someone close to me says. I wish they'd all stay put
and not wander back here.

"So, I just wanted to say," the close-by voice says. *Who is he talking to? It's like he's right on top of me.*

I sneak a peek out from under my arm, and I see Matt. I lift my head.

He's not talking to anybody, though.

No, I mean, he is. He's talking to me.

"I just hadn't really thought about those things until you said them," he's saying. "And you were right about Silas. I sat with him on the bus today so I could apologize, and he wasn't anything like I had been thinking."

I open my mouth but nothing comes out.

"So, I just wanted to say," Matt continues, "that I'm sorry and that you should come back to the debate club. You're really good at it."

I quickly look away and shake my head. "You're the kind of person who should be in the debate club. Someone who can be confident without getting so upset that they knock over a cardboard cutout of Harry Potter. Like when you gave that speech before the student council election, totally professional."

I glance at him and he's looking more uncomfortable than I think I've ever seen him.

"Can I tell you a secret?" he whispers.

I look up. Is he blushing?

"What?" I say.

"My mom wrote that speech for me."

"She did?"

"Yeah. It was easy to be calm since it was a good speech, and since most of the people watching were my friends."

"Your mom really wrote that for you?" I still can't get over that.

"Yeah, is that wrong? I figured it was a better speech than I could have written, and people deserved a good speech, so . . . " He trails off. "That was probably wrong, wasn't it?"

I shrug. "I just can't imagine my mom ever writing a student council election speech for me."

"I just wanted people to like the speech, you know?"

"Yeah, I know."

"But that's why you should come back to debate club because you don't need your mom to write a speech for you. You don't even need notes. Lydia wants you to come back, too. Because you just say what you think, you know? And that's really cool."

I try to picture going back to debate club. Could I really do it? Wait—did Matt Hubbard just call me cool?

"Like, really," he continues, "I think I'd score better points at the tournament if I could be more like you were on Friday."

I look at him. At his nicely combed hair. At his pleading brown eyes. At his complete cluelessness that somehow it all comes down to how many points you can score in a tournament.

I take a deep breath. "I think that sometimes you need to have your back up against the wall to find out what you're made of. And you just haven't had that happen to you yet."

Matt nods like he totally gets what I'm saying and that maybe you can order a having-your-back-up-against-the-wall experience online and have it delivered to your house.

"You know what could be good to do?" I say. Because if somehow the world has turned upside down and I, Zoey Albro, am giving Matt Hubbard advice, then I might as well keep going. "If you imagine what it's like to have your back up against the wall all the time, you might be less likely to assume someone's stupid and evil." I glance down at the desk. "Especially someone like Silas."

I never see Silas during the school day except at lunch, but usually he's in mute mode so that doesn't really count.

Today is different because when I'm on my way to the hot lunch line, I see him crossing the cafeteria. And he's coming right over to me.

"Where were you this morning?" he asks. With words, out loud words.

People are streaming past us on their way to the line. "It's kind of complicated," I say. "We kind of moved."

"Moved? But Lenny's car was still there last night."

"Moved without Lenny," I say. "Moved because of Lenny." Silas bites his lip and nods. "Oh . . . " He studies the cafeteria floor. "Matt Hubbard talked to me on the bus this morning. He said you said something about me at debate club."

"I'm sorry," I say quickly. "It wasn't really my business, but I—"

"Thanks," he says. He's looking up at me now and his freckles want me to connect them into rainbows and unicorns. "Matt and I talked for a while. It was cool."

I look away from his freckles. "Did you tell Matt about bobcat hunting?"

"No. Why?"

Because it's our special secret, that's why! "No reason."

"You know, my dad and I are going back out to scout Squaretail Brook again early on Sunday." He steps to the side to get out of someone's way. "The bobcat hunting season ended last week, but I still want to find some sign of it. Something to prove that it's really there."

I study the fake wood pattern in the closest cafeteria table and try not to show how much I suddenly wish I could be scouting Squaretail Brook with him.

"You know, it's cool that you're doing debate club," Silas says. "That takes lots of guts."

I shake my head. "I just did it for a few weeks. I don't know if I'm going to go back." I follow the concentric circles of the fake wood as they get bigger and bigger.

"Well, it sounded like you were pretty good at it based on what Matt said."

I keep my eyes glued to the table. Did he really just say that?

"So, when am I going to see you?" Silas asks.

He couldn't have just said that.

"Hey, Zoey. Hey, Silas."

I look up to see Matt walking past on his way to the lunch line.

Kaylee is right behind him. "Did you seriously just say hi to them?" she hisses loud enough for me to hear.

Matt glances back at me. "Yeah. Why shouldn't I?"

They keep walking.

"Zoey, are you okay?" Silas asks.

My face must be a total mess of disbelief.

I take a deep breath and look at Silas with his hazel eyes and unicorns made of freckles. "Yes. I am." I take a second deep breath. Then, I rip a piece of paper out of my math notebook. "This is my mom's cell phone number. Maybe we could meet up after school sometime?"

Silas stares at the paper I'm handing him and then takes it. "Thanks."

I swallow down all of the nerves trying to erupt out of me. "Like maybe could I come with you and your dad when you go scouting for bobcats?"

He looks up at me. "How about Sunday morning?"

I manage a nod. "That'd be great."

When I'm sitting in English class an hour later I realize I

should probably keep going to debate club meetings, too. And that I could sit next to Kyla.

Because I'm pretty sure she knows what it's like to have your back up against the wall—and it's always good to stick together.

I get to social studies class early, and Ms. Rochambeau is up out of her chair as soon as she sees me.

"Zoey. I've been meaning to talk to you. I'm so glad you said what you did at that last debate club practice. What I need to know now is: Are you safe?

"What do you mean?"

"You talked about an adult intimidating a girl with a gun. Was that you?"

I shake my head. "It wasn't." Half of me wants to spit out Fuchsia's name, but the rest of me knows enough to keep it locked up tight.

"Are you sure? Are you sure that you're safe?"

"I am. I wasn't before, but it wasn't because of a gun. It was because of a guy, a different guy." I look up at her. "A guy who was really good at discrediting his opponent."

Ms. Rochambeau exhales and sits back down in her chair. "Tell me."

I glance at the door and see other kids starting to arrive. "The main thing is that you helped me see what he was doing. I realized that I didn't have to look at things the way he wanted."

Ms. Rochambeau's face changes. I think she's trying to keep from crying. She nods and then wipes her eyes and pulls me into a hug. "If anyone could do it, it was you, Zoey."

When she finally releases me she looks at me. "So, will you come back to debate club?"

I swallow. "I have to help my friend today, but I promise I'll be there tomorrow." I hesitate. "Can you still drive me? I live somewhere else now."

"I'll drive you wherever you need to go, Zoey. And listen." She takes a form off her desk and slips it into my hand. "I'll be handing out these debate tournament entry forms today after school, and I want you to seriously think about it. The fees will be covered. All you'd need to bring is yourself." She raises her eyebrows and smiles at me. "And your willingness to speak up."

I bite back a smile. On my way to my seat, I don't throw the form in the trash. I don't even drop it in the paper recycling. Instead, I tuck it into my pocket.

CHAPTER 28

In the afternoon I take the bus with Fuchsia, and we get off two stops early at the police department so she can drop off the paperwork that Crystal finally agreed to fill out to keep Michael away. When we get to Fuchsia's apartment, my mom has already left for work—but since Crystal is done with her early shift at the bakery by 1:30 p.m., she agreed to watch Hector until I get home from school.

"I can take Hector with me to go meet Bryce and Aurora at their new bus stop. I'm used to that," I say.

Crystal eyes Hector with all of the take-out containers on the floor. "Okay."

I heft him onto my hip. "You know the drill, little man. You're coming with me." He pulls at my hair. I nuzzle my nose into the side of his face and reach for the door.

"Wait," Crystal says, opening the fridge. "I'm supposed to let you know that these are in here. Your mom got them for you guys."

There are nine perfect yogurt containers lined up on the refrigerator shelf.

"And she put a stack of clean laundry on the bed for you."

I look at Crystal, but she just shrugs like between letting me know about this and watching Hector, she's hit her maternal limit.

"Thank you," I say.

I slip out the door before my eyes can tear up more.

A few hours later, Bryce, Aurora, Fuchsia, Crystal, and I have all eaten a yogurt and also some day-old pastry bear claws that Crystal produced from her bag. Even Hector got to stick his fist into a yogurt before I realized what was happening. Someday when he's a grown-up one-year-old he'll look back on this time without his ExerSaucer as the good old days when he was naked and free. Too bad for him I've got plans to check the free exchange spot at the dump this weekend. They always have a broken ExerSaucer or two, and it's going to bring Hector's yogurt-covered party to an end.

It's Bryce who I'm most worried about. When he woke up

from those nightmares last night, he was soaked through with sweat and it was like he couldn't wake up enough to realize that it wasn't real. And how do you get inside someone's head to help them when they're wrapped up in fear like that?

Especially because both me and him would know that I'd be lying if I said that everything's going to be fine now that we've moved.

The garbage bags are now in the bedroom and I dig through one of them, trying not to let stuff fall out and make a mess on the floor. Finally, my hand closes around the thin plastic rectangle that I'm looking for and I pull it out. The Mickey Mouse night-light.

I plug it in, and call to Bryce and Aurora. "Do you want a story tonight?"

"'Tory! 'Tory! 'Tory!" Aurora cries, bouncing into the room with Jane Kitty clutched in her hands like Godzilla with its hostage.

Bryce comes in more hesitantly.

"Do you want help changing into your pajamas?" I ask.

He shakes his head, but then he just sits down on the new mattress that's squeezed against the wall.

"Here." I find his pajamas in the pile where he left them in the morning, and help him out of his shirt. "Do you want to listen to a story?" I pull his threadbare pajama shirt over his head.

He shrugs. I help him switch from jeans to pajama pants.

"That's cozier, right?" I put my arm around him and scooch us back farther onto the mattress. Aurora, who has already put on her Hello Kitty nightgown comes over and plants herself on my lap. Hector is busy emptying all of our things out of one of the trash bags, so that should occupy him for a while.

I'm just about to start telling a story when Fuchsia comes into the bedroom.

"Are we in your way?" I ask.

She shakes her head but just stands there, looking at us awkwardly.

"I was going to tell them a story," I say.

"Yeah, I heard." Fuchsia bites her lip. "Can I listen, too?"

Suddenly Aurora is out of my lap, clearing off random clothes from the mattress. "You can come 'nuggle, too!" she cries. "There's lots of 'pace."

Fuchsia looks at me and then quickly looks away. Still, she lowers herself onto the mattress in the glow of the Mickey Mouse night-light and settles in.

I start in on the story. It's about some kids floating around in the ocean far away from land, and there are sharks—so many sharks. But they manage to find some pieces of wood floating nearby. And the kids gang up together, and with the biggest pieces of wood they can find they all whack those sharks on the head until they stop circling. And then they drag all of their pieces of wood together and use rope to build a huge awesome raft. The raft has a little spot where they can cook their food, stairs going up to a loft where they can sleep, and great views of the sunrise.

I've been rubbing Bryce's back, and he turns to look at me. "Where's the kids' mom?"

I swallow. "You can't always see her, but she's there. She's been swimming underwater, trying to find every piece of wood she can for her kids, doing everything she can to help them survive."

Bryce nods and leans back against me. After a long moment, he says, "How many people are in the water?"

I glance at Fuchsia. "There are a lot of people in the water."

"So then, they need to make the raft big enough so everyone can fit on it, right?" he says.

"Well," I say slowly. "I'm sure they'll make it as big as they can. They'll use every single piece of wood that they have."

Aurora looks up from where she's been lying in my lap, twirling her hair around her finger. "Maybe the other people in the water have wood, too. They can help make the raft bigger!"

I wrap my octopus tentacles around both of them. "Maybe they do."

Or maybe I have it all wrong. The ocean is a fine place to live for an octopus. And maybe it's all those people who are spending their whole lives up on dry land—never once going into the water to see what it feels like—who are missing out.

I keep rubbing Bryce's back until he slumps forward and curls up around Aurora. Two tired, little monkeys.

And both of those tired, little monkeys sleep through the night—without waking up from a nightmare once.

But I stay awake for hours. Because I'm suddenly bursting with stories. Not made-up stories. Real ones. I guess they're actually not stories if they're real things that happen to real people. They are: Things That Need To Be Said.

Out loud.

At debate club.

So those other kids can hear it.

By morning, I've even filled out the entry form for the debate tournament and put it in my backpack. Because I'm going. And I'm going to speak up. No matter how scary it is.

ACKNOWLEDGMENTS

This book would not exist if it weren't for a village of amaz-ing people. Like Elizabeth Immergut, who was concerned that her students living in rural poverty didn't see themselves enough in books and turned to me and told me to write this. Like Pamela Simmons, who inspired me by "finding her brave" and speaking out about her experience with domestic violence. I watched her reclaim her voice and found out exactly how strong people could be.

I am grateful to all the conversations and voices that helped me make this book as honest as I could. I am grateful to those who were willing to share their stories in all the books and first-person accounts that I read. I am grateful to (and in awe of) those who are standing on the front lines working to create a world where everyone is respected and safe: Donna

Macomber, Karen Tronsgard-Scott, Auburn Watersong, Clai Lasher-Sommers, Elissa Pine, Sharon Panitch, Melissa Weinstein, and so many others. They are brave, and they channel a powerful, fierce love in everything they do.

I am grateful to the gun owners who have helped me understand the complexities of gun issues, especially the students who told me about their great hunting trips and Ryan Hockertlotz who showed me how to shoot.

There are incredible writers who have made this book better, been a support network, and served as an ongoing source of inspiration . . . I am thankful for Tara Dairman, Elaine Vickers, Jennifer Chambliss Bertman, Jessica Lawson, Joy McCullough, Tamara Ellis Smith, Kari Anne Holt, Jeannie Mobley, Jennifer Stewart, Kip Wilson, Josephine Cameron, and Sarah Ellis . . . for their honesty, for their vulnerability, and for their brilliance. And for the entire EMLA family who believed in me and told me I was a writer.

I am grateful to the incredible librarians I've worked with over the years: Brenda Durrin, Ellen Nosal, Mary Linney, Paige Martin, Lindsay Bellville, Jeanne Walsh, and Starr Latronica. I liked books a lot when I was a kid, but I didn't love them . . . until I met all of you. And to all of those in the Nerdy Book Club community, between your love for books and your love for children you're making such positive change in the world. Please keep fanning those flames—because it's contagious.

I am grateful for Kirsten Cappy, who shaped pivotal

moments in this story and inspires me with her determination to make the world a better place by getting good books into readers' hands.

I am indebted to my editor, Becky Herrick, for her vision, her steady hand, and her devotion to these characters and the core of this story. This book would not be the book it is without her.

Whenever you fly your heart out into the world, it's so helpful to have people who believe in you no matter what, who can provide the firm ground that forms your launching pad. I am so thankful to have my agent Tricia Lawrence at my side. She gave me the courage to approach this story with honesty first and to let everything else follow.

I do not have enough words to thank my husband Dan, who has cheered me on at every turn and been so supportive of my need to write. He is both my rock and my source for the deep belly laughs that restore my soul.

I would like to thank my children, Ethan and Alice, for all the times they've been patient with me when I "just have to finish this sentence" and for inspiring me to write toward a better world.

Finally, this book is dedicated to my mom, who raised me by herself and taught me how much strength there can be below the surface of a person. She is the steady bow that sent my arrow flying.

To single parents everywhere doing the best they can for their kids . . .

To the young people who are speaking up for what's right, even when it's hard . . .

You are heroes.